"Ask me to stay," Travis said.

Sara sucked in a deep breath and exhaled slowly.

"Stay," she whispered. *I must be crazy.* Sara stared at her and Travis's reflection in the hall mirror. Her dress made her feel beautiful and desirable—but would she feel that way once it came off? Or would Travis see the plain Jane everyone in town saw?

Her gaze collided with Travis's in the mirror and the heat in his eyes reassured her.

He slid a finger beneath her dress strap and moved it aside. She shivered at the feel of his fingertips on her skin.

"What are you afraid of?" he asked.

"Nothing." *Everything.* Women like her didn't win the hearts of fantasy men like Travis. He was out of her league.

Travis brushed aside a strand of hair clinging to her cheek. "Fess up, Sara Sanders, because when I get you upstairs there's not going to be any room in that bed for doubts."

Dear Reader,

Welcome back to Tulapoint, Oklahoma. When I began writing about the Cartwright siblings in *The Cowboy and the Angel* (November 2008), *A Cowboy's Promise* (April 2009) and *Samantha's Cowboy* (August 2009), I had no idea there would be a fourth sibling. Then my imagination took off. What if there was another son—a son the family never knew existed?

I wondered how I'd feel if one day I learned that the father I was led to believe wanted nothing to do with me, never even knew I'd existed. American Romance is all about family. When family dynamics suddenly change in a dramatic way, everyone's lives are thrown into chaos. Travis's struggle to claim his rightful place in the family encounters a snag when he falls for Sara—his father's neighbor and longtime nemesis. Travis is torn between wanting to please his father and being with the one woman he trusts his heart with. Then Travis and Sara discover the secret responsible for the years of bad feelings between the families. Will their love be enough to heal the pain and bring both families together?

I hope you enjoy visiting the Cartwright family one last time. For more information on my books and to sign up for my newsletter please visit www.marinthomas.com. Information on Harlequin American Romance authors and their books can be found at www.harauthors.blogspot.com.

And if you like rodeo cowboys, get ready for my new Harlequin American Romance series…Rodeo Rebels! Look for *Rodeo Daddy* available in April 2011.

Yippie yi yay!

Marin

Roughneck Cowboy
Marin Thomas

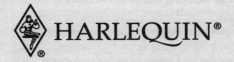

HARLEQUIN®

TORONTO • NEW YORK • LONDON
AMSTERDAM • PARIS • SYDNEY • HAMBURG
STOCKHOLM • ATHENS • TOKYO • MILAN • MADRID
PRAGUE • WARSAW • BUDAPEST • AUCKLAND

Recycling programs
for this product may
not exist in your area.

ISBN-13: 978-0-373-75345-1

ROUGHNECK COWBOY

Copyright © 2011 by Brenda Smith-Beagley

www.eHarlequin.com

Printed in U.S.A.

ABOUT THE AUTHOR

Marin Thomas grew up in Janesville, Wisconsin. She attended the University of Arizona in Tucson on a Division I basketball scholarship. In 1986 she graduated with a B.A. in radio-television and married her college sweetheart in a five-minute ceremony in Las Vegas. Marin was inducted in May 2005 into the Janesville Sports Hall of Fame for her basketball accomplishments. Even though she now calls Chicago home, she's a living testament to the old adage "You can take the girl out of the small town, but you can't take the small town out of the girl." Marin's heart still lies in small-town life, which she loves to write about in her books.

Books by Marin Thomas

HARLEQUIN AMERICAN ROMANCE

1024—THE COWBOY AND THE BRIDE
1050—DADDY BY CHOICE
1079—HOMEWARD BOUND
1124—AARON UNDER CONSTRUCTION*
1148—NELSON IN COMMAND*
1165—SUMMER LOVIN'
       "The Preacher's Daughter"
1175—RYAN'S RENOVATION*
1184—FOR THE CHILDREN**
1200—IN A SOLDIER'S ARMS**
1224—A COAL MINER'S WIFE**
1236—THE COWBOY AND THE ANGEL
1253—A COWBOY'S PROMISE
1271—SAMANTHA'S COWBOY
1288—A COWBOY CHRISTMAS
1314—DEXTER: HONORABLE COWBOY

*The McKade Brothers
**Hearts of Appalachia

To my niece, Tylesha

Find your inspiration—
the one thing that feeds your soul.
That makes you yearn to be more than you
ever imagined you could be. Chase after it
and don't look back. There will be times you
want to give up. *Don't.* Dig harder. Longer. Deeper.
The good stuff is always at the bottom.
Everything you need to succeed is already inside you.
Believe in yourself and dream big.

Chapter One

"I gotta use the bathroom, Dad."

Well, shoot. Lost in thought, Travis Cartwright had all but forgotten that his eight-year-old daughter, Charlie, rode in the front seat with him. They'd departed Houston, Texas, hours ago and she'd yet to release the glower from her face.

He sucked at fatherhood and had no one to blame but himself. His job as a roughneck kept him separated from his daughter for weeks on end, then whenever he returned to the mainland, he spent most of his time catching up on sleep and yard work.

"Keep an eye out for a place to stop." Another ten miles and they'd clear the outskirts of Tulsa, Oklahoma. From there they'd drive northwest until they reached their final destination—the Lazy River Ranch. "I'm hungry. How about you, kiddo?"

One shoulder, no bigger than the bottom of a coffee mug, lifted, remained elevated a second, then dropped back into place. Her elfin face stared straight ahead, pale eyelashes blinking rhythmically in time with the windshield wipers.

Keep trying. "Snow's coming down faster." As dusk descended, flakes danced in the truck's headlights and ribbons of white swirled across the road. Was he nuts for making this trip two days before Thanksgiving? "Maybe there'll be enough snow to play in tomorrow morning."

"I hate snow."

Not the greatest attitude, but he'd take words over a shrug any day. Charlie was nothing more than an imp—a blond-headed sprite with blue eyes. He'd called her Twinkie as a toddler. Dripping wet, his daughter didn't weigh more than forty-five pounds. What Charlie lacked in size she made up for in pure stubbornness.

Charlie inherited her slight build and fair coloring from her mother. Julie had split right after Charlie's birth and hadn't bothered to leave a forwarding address. Lucky for him Travis's mother, Charlotte, had been there to help him raise Charlie.

I'm sorry, Travis. So sorry. His mother's dying words clanged around inside his brain. He squeezed his eyes shut, then opened them wide. Silence—*thank God.* Since her death, his mother's voice had been a constant presence in his head.

"Maybe your grandfather has horses."

The question thunked between him and Charlie like a boulder hitting the pavement. Travis strangled the steering wheel, recalling how often his mother had cautioned him that, if he didn't pay more attention to his daughter, they'd grow apart. He'd heard the warnings but had ignored them. He'd counted on his mother always being there for him and Charlie and for there always being another time or another day to spend with his daughter.

Well, *another time* and *another day* had arrived and were right now chasing his anxious ass down an

Oklahoma highway. "I bet there's a dog on the ranch." They'd never owned a pet, because his mother had been allergic to animal fur. Fortunately, a neighbor allowed Charlie to play with his golden retriever, and that was almost as good as having her own dog. "There's probably a cat or two in the barn."

More shrugs.

He yearned to reassure his daughter that everything would be okay, but feared neither one of them would emerge from the wreckage of Charlotte Cartwright's death without scars—how many and how deep time would tell. Two weeks ago, he'd taken a leave of absence from his job as a roughneck on the Exxon Mobil Hoover Diana and had sat by his dying mother's bedside, listening to her perplexing apology before she'd slipped away.

More than his mother's death had shaken the foundation of his and Charlie's world. When Travis had gone through his mother's personal property, he'd discovered a diary—Pandora's box. Suddenly Charlotte's apology had made perfect sense.

His mother's secret had turned Travis's world upside down and spurred the journey he and his daughter had embarked upon. On the yellowed pages of flower-patterned stationery, Travis had learned the identity of his father—famous Oklahoma oil baron Dominick Cartwright.

Travis's gut burned with anger and resentment toward both parents. He assumed his mother had kept his father a secret all these years to protect him from rejection. Still, the choice to know his father or not should have been Travis's, and he was determined to learn why his father wanted nothing to do with him.

When Travis had done an internet search for Dominick Cartwright, the more information he'd uncovered, the angrier he'd become. He'd welcomed the anger. Better resentment than hurt—he was a roughneck, for God's sake. Slaving away on an oil platform in the middle of the ocean in dangerous, harsh conditions should have toughened his hide and made it impossible to care one way or the other about his father's disregard. No such luck. Add in the strange sense of relief he'd felt at learning he and his daughter weren't alone in the world, and he was one confused, messed-up roughneck.

Charlotte's death had also left Charlie in a vulnerable position. Travis had considered quitting his job in order to be home with his daughter, but he was in line for a promotion and without a college education he'd never make as much money on the mainland. Regardless, his position on the rig was risky—the Deepwater Horizon catastrophe in the Gulf of Mexico the previous year was proof of that.

With Charlie's grandmother out of the picture, Travis worried that if he were to die while his daughter was young, she'd become a ward of the state. He'd decided to make the trip to Oklahoma for Charlie's sake, not his. He didn't need a relationship with his estranged father nor the brother and sister his mother had written about in her diary.

Yeah, right. Keep telling yourself that and maybe you'll believe it.

Dominick had better not turn his back on his granddaughter—the man owed Travis for not claiming him all these years.

Rather than admit an attack of nerves had invaded

his intestines, he blamed his queasy stomach on the fact that he hadn't eaten in hours. Like a pendulum, his gaze swung back and forth across the road, searching for a place to eat and pee—as Charlie put it.

A Victorian house sprang up in the middle of nowhere and he pulled onto the shoulder of the road. He studied the pink-and-black monstrosity surrounded by an iron gate. Travis wondered if he'd stumbled upon a backwoods bordello.

"Beulah's," he said.

Charlie wrinkled her nose. "Huh?"

"The sign in the front yard says Beulah's."

"What's a Beulah?"

"A restaurant, I think." Travis turned into the driveway alongside the home and drove to the back of the lot where three pickups and one patrol car were parked. Patio tables covered in a dusting of snow sat in the backyard and a Welcome sign hung on the door.

Travis turned off the ignition and unbuckled his seat belt. "Let's see if Beulah has a bathroom you can use."

Charlie didn't budge.

Most parents wouldn't tolerate obstinacy, but he allowed his daughter's behavior to slide. To his way of thinking, he deserved her sullenness. He'd been absent more than present during Charlie's young life—even missed a few of her birthdays because he hadn't been able to switch his shift on the platform. It would take time for him and Charlie to find their way without Grandma Charlotte to guide them.

When he opened the door, the smell of fried burgers and crisp evening air filled his lungs. His stomach growled loudly. Charlie took her dang tootin' time getting out of the truck, but he kept a lid on his temper and pretended to enjoy the balmy thirty-two-degree temperature.

A clunky cowbell attached to the door handle announced their arrival when they entered the Victorian.

"Welcome to Beulah's!" An older woman with a 1960s beehive hairdo dyed pitch-black and wearing a pink muumuu and house slippers greeted them. "I'm Beulah. We got a few tables left in the front room." She motioned for them to follow her through the house.

With a hand on his daughter's shoulder, Travis guided Charlie down the hall and into the dining area. All three tables in the room were occupied. They followed Beulah across the foyer and into the parlor, which boasted a fireplace. He and Charlie sat at the table near the windows.

Beulah handed them a laminated handwritten menu. "Special's leftovers."

Leftovers?

"With Thanksgiving right around the corner, I'm cleaning out the fridge." Beulah batted her false eyelashes and smiled at Charlie. "You sure are a pipsqueak."

Travis winced. Charlie hated people commenting on her small stature.

"Just 'cause I'm little don't mean—"

"Doesn't," Travis interrupted.

Charlie glared at him. "—doesn't mean I'm stupid."

Beulah's charcoal eyebrows arched into her hairline. "I never said nothing about you having trouble with your brain. For all I know, you might grow up to be the next president of these here United States."

Before his daughter caused a ruckus with the restaurant owner, Travis asked, "Do you have a restroom Charlie can use?"

"Next to the kitchen. I'll show you." Beulah escorted his scowling daughter away.

A short time later, Charlie returned. While she played with the salt-and-pepper shakers, he perused the handwritten menu. Chicken fingers wasn't one of the leftover specials. "Think you might want to try the rice casserole?"

"Yuck."

Thought so. "What about a hamburger?"

"Double yuck."

"What about—"

"A bowl of cereal?" Beulah stopped at the table.

"What kind?" Charlie asked.

"Froot Loops."

"You have really tall hair." Charlie gaped at Beulah's beehive.

"Twelve inches worth of it, sweetheart. You eating cereal or not?"

"I like Froot Loops."

Beulah nodded at Travis. "You?"

"I'll have a burger. Medium well."

"Drinks?"

"A glass of milk for Charlie. Coffee for me."

"Comin' right up." Beulah shoved the pencil into her hair chimney, took two steps, then stopped. "Where are you folks from?"

"Houston."

"Passing through or visiting?"

"We're going to see my grandpa." Charlie's eyes

welled with tears. "'Cause I don't have a mom and my grandma just died."

Travis felt like he'd been punched in the windpipe. During the past week, his daughter had been so brave. She hadn't cried in front of him, but he'd stood outside her bedroom door at night feeling helpless as he listened to her muffled sniffles.

"Ah, honey." Beulah brushed a strand of blond hair off Charlie's forehead. "I'm sorry about your mama and your grandma." She sent an apologetic smile Travis's way.

The bell on the back door clanged and Beulah rushed off. A minute later, a tall, plain-looking woman entered the parlor. Bundled in a long, brown coat, she clutched a bulging tote bag to her chest. Snowflakes dotted her shoulder-length dark hair, the white specks melting into water beads that sparkled in the firelight. She set the tote on the floor, draped her coat over the back of her chair, then sat down. Her eyes skipped over him, but when she spotted Charlie, she smiled. Travis waited for her to make eye contact with him, but instead she rummaged through the tote on the floor.

Travis wasn't a vain man, but working on an oil rig in the middle of the ocean gave him a year-round tan and a muscular physique. Add in his dark black hair and killer smile and, more often than not, women noticed him. He wasn't sure if he should protest or laugh that he'd been passed over by plain Jane.

"Food will be right up," Beulah said, poking her head into the room. She switched her attention to the newcomer. "Sara, don't you ever take a break from grading papers?"

So plain Jane was a schoolteacher.

The lady chuckled at Beulah's comment, the husky sound conjuring up an image of a late-night necking session in the backseat of Travis's truck. That he'd find anything interesting about a woman who wasn't his usual type reminded Travis his love life of late had been dryer than Death Valley.

He'd had one long-term relationship in his thirty years—Charlie's mother. They'd dated for three years before Julie had become pregnant. He'd suggested they marry but Julie found one excuse after another to avoid a trip to the courthouse. A week after they'd brought Charlie home from the hospital, Julie had ditched them.

No note. No call. Just gone.

After Julie's betrayal, Travis had stuck to flings. His two-week work rotation on oil rigs made trusting a girl-friend out of the question. Affairs were clean, quick and emotionless. And right now, Travis had bigger problems than his love life. Once he took care of business with Dominick Cartwright, his first priority was finding a nanny to care for Charlie.

Once in a while Travis pondered what his life might be like if he didn't have Charlie to raise. Most days she was a good kid and he never regretted being a single father—mainly because his mother had done most of the parenting. Now the full responsibility of raising Charlie sat squarely on his shoulders and he'd never felt more unprepared for anything in his life.

"Here you go," Beulah said, delivering their food. She tweaked Charlie's nose, coaxing a half-smile from her. "Holler if you need anything else."

He took a bite of the burger and watched Charlie as

she spooned cereal into her mouth. "How are the Froot Loops?"

Another shrug. The rest of the meal passed in silence. When Travis finished his burger, he said, "I'm going to use the restroom." He made it to the doorway when the schoolteacher's sultry laughter rang out. He checked over his shoulder, but the woman was engrossed in the schoolwork she'd brought with her. Maybe he'd imagined the sound.

When he entered the restroom, he did a three-sixty in front of the mirror. No embarrassing stains or rips in his jeans. No *kick me* note stuck to his sweatshirt. What had the schoolteacher found so damned funny?

WHEN THE HUNKY MAN returned to the parlor, Sara pretended interest in her second-graders' spelling tests. Through veiled eyes, she studied the man, noting his bare ring finger. She wondered if he was the little girl's father. Uncle? Family friend? The absence of a bow-legged walk confirmed he was no cowboy, but his muscular build and deeply tanned face suggested he made his living outdoors.

The imp fidgeted in her seat, peeking at Sara every few seconds. *Oh, dear.* The child realized she had an audience. When Beulah delivered her meal, Sara nodded toward the other diners and whispered, "Who are they?"

"Came up from Houston to visit the little girl's granddaddy." Beulah motioned to Sara's coffee mug. "More?"

"Thanks."

Sara had just taken a bite of corn bread when Mr. Coppertone bent to pick up his napkin from the floor.

The girl stuck out her tongue, wiggling the appendage like a worm on a fishhook. Sara giggled, but looked away before the child caught her staring. Her resolve to ignore the comedian lasted less than a minute. When she glanced up, two white straws protruded from the girl's nose. Sara awarded her an A for creativity—the walrus face was priceless.

The man stopped playing with his cell phone and scowled. "That's not funny, Charlie."

Charlie. Unusual name for a girl.

"Take the straws out of your nose." His deep voice boomed. "Now."

The troublemaker pointed at Sara. "She thinks I'm funny."

Oh, you little stinker. Sara resisted the urge to duck her head. She offered a friendly smile, but the man's scowl remained in place.

"I don't care if the world thinks you're hilarious. Finish your cereal."

"I want to go home." The pint-size rascal crossed her arms over her chest and pouted.

"Too late to turn back now. We're in this for keeps."

His words coaxed a quiet sigh from Sara. What she wouldn't give to find a handsome man who wanted to be in it for keeps with *her*.

THE GRAVEL ROAD LEADING to the Lazy River Ranch felt like a dark, endless tunnel. Travis battled another round of second thoughts as they bumped along the path. Should he have phoned and given the old man a heads-up about his and Charlie's visit? Or should he have waited until after the holidays to drop in? He shoved his worries aside. Dominick Cartwright didn't deserve any courtesies from him.

What if your father didn't know you existed all these years?

Travis had considered the possibility, but it was easier to assume Dominick had wanted nothing to do with him than to believe his mother—the woman who'd raised him single-handedly all these years—had denied him a relationship with his father.

"When are we gonna be there?"

No sooner had Charlie spoken than the ranch house came into view. Halogen lights lit the circular drive crowded with cars. Damn, he'd crashed a party. He parked by the empty coral.

From a distance, the barn appeared old but in pristine condition. He'd have expected an oil baron to possess a state-of-the-art aluminum-sided structure with central air and all the high-tech stuff. Maybe the small cattle herd they'd driven past was just for show. He switched his attention to the house. Light poured through the windows of the white two-story home with a wrap-around porch.

"Well, I'll be," he mumbled when a hound dog limped from around the corner of the house.

Charlie unsnapped her seat belt and pressed her nose to the windshield. "What's wrong with him?"

"Probably just old."

"He looks sad."

The dog barked once, swished its tail, then disappeared inside the barn. "I guess that means we're welcome."

"Aren't we going in?" Charlie asked.

How did a father explain to his little girl that he was scared spitless?

You're doing this for Charlie.

If he could fool himself into believing that, then he wouldn't have to acknowledge his own need to know if he'd ever mattered to the man who'd sired him. The decision to stay or leave was taken out of his hands when the front door opened and two men stepped outside. They stood beneath the porch light and stared in Travis's direction. A moment later, they shuffled down the steps and headed across the driveway.

"Stay put, Charlie." Travis cut the engine and got out of the truck. One man walked with a cowboy swagger, the other possessed the steady gait of a confident businessman.

As they drew near, the swaggering cowboy spoke. "Need directions?"

Hardly. "I'm here to see Dominick Cartwright."

Both men stopped a few yards away. Travis didn't blame them for being cautious. He suspected all kinds of kooks claimed they had business with Dominick Cartwright in hopes of getting their hands on his millions. "Got a name?" the businessman asked.

"Travis Cartwright from Houston, Texas."

Right then the front door opened again and an elderly gentleman stepped outside. There was no doubt in Travis's mind that the man was Dominick Cartwright. He stood tall and straight with dark hair and a white mustache. "Matt? What's going on out there?" He headed toward the group.

"Duke and I will take care of it, Dad!" the cowboy shouted.

Travis's mother hadn't mentioned a third child in her

diary entries, so he had no idea who Duke was, but the cowboy must be Matt—his mother had mentioned an older brother by that name. As his father drew closer, Travis suddenly wanted to run. To pretend he'd never learned of his mother's secret. To reject the idea that he was part of a family he hadn't known existed most of his life.

Charlie hopped out of the truck and joined Travis, sliding her hand into his. He squeezed his daughter's fingers embarrassed by the need for her support.

Despite the fact that there must be more than thirty years difference in their ages, the old man's chiseled face was a dead ringer for the one that met Travis in the mirror each morning. They shared the same nose, high cheekbones and thick, black eyebrows. If there was any doubt, the pronounced Adam's apple sealed the deal.

"Dominick Cartwright?" Travis said, cursing the break in his voice.

The old man stiffened. "Who are you?"

Disappointment stabbed Travis, but he squelched the feeling. Now was not the time to *feel*. "Travis Cartwright. According to my mother, Charlotte Keegan-Cartwright, I'm your son."

Dominick stumbled back and the other men steadied him. Masculine hands covered in a network of thick veins clenched into fists. He opened his mouth, then shut it so tightly his lips vanished beneath the mustache as he stared at Travis.

Unfazed by the tension between the adults, Charlie asked, "Are you my grandpa?"

Before Dominick had a chance to answer, Duke said, "Help Dad inside, Matt."

Travis's brother took Dominick's arm and led him

away. Once the two were out of earshot, Duke said, "You better be for real or you'll have a lot to answer for."

Travis nodded toward the house, where a group of women and children had gathered on the front porch. "I don't want to intrude. Charlie and I will return in a couple of days."

"No one drops a bomb like you just did and walks away. C'mon."

He was grateful Charlie hadn't released his hand as they followed Duke. If he wasn't so agitated, he'd laugh at himself—the big, bad roughneck afraid of a few rich people.

"What's the matter, Duke?" one of the women asked when they neared the porch steps.

"We'll talk inside."

The crowd filed into the house, then Duke motioned Travis and Charlie ahead of him. They joined the others in the crowded foyer. Dominick stood to the side, staring into space.

After a tense silence, Charlie blurted, "How come no one's talking?"

A pregnant woman with blond hair smiled. "I'm Renée." She set her hand on the shoulder of a young boy. "This is my son, Timmy." The woman motioned across the foyer. "You've met my husband, Duke."

A tall woman with long black hair and a quizzical expression stepped forward. "I'm Samantha."

My sister. Travis and Samantha shared the same dark eyebrows, olive skin and jet-black hair. Unlike his brother, Matt, whose blue eyes, brown hair and paler complexion favored their mother.

Samantha slipped her arm through the man's next

to her and hugged a little boy close. Both males wore identical eyeglasses. "My husband, Wade, and our son, Luke."

"I'm Amy, Matt's wife." A petite woman with curly hair motioned to two little girls. "Our daughters, Rose and Lily." The girls giggled and hid behind their mother's legs.

"I'm Charlie."

"That's a weird name for a girl," the boy wearing glasses said.

"Charlie's my nickname."

"What's your real name?" the boy asked.

"Charlotte. That's my grandma's name, too."

The adults froze at Charlie's announcement.

"Where's your grandma?" the little girl in pigtails asked.

"She died. And I don't have a mom. It's just me and my dad now." Charlie fidgeted next to Travis, unaware of the bombshell she'd dropped.

Samantha slapped a hand over her mouth and tears flooded her eyes. Matt's face drained of color. Travis searched out Dominick, but the old man had disappeared. A moment later, the echo of a slamming door thundered through the hallway.

Chapter Two

Travis wasn't sure if his physical presence or the news of his mother's death had caused his estranged father to leave the group. Regardless, Travis decided he wasn't ready for this confrontation. "Charlie, let's go."

"Wait." The blond woman named Renée stepped forward. "We were about to serve dessert. Please stay."

"Last one to the kitchen's a rotten egg." Timmy took off, and the other kids followed. Renée held out her hand to Charlie.

Noticing Samantha's pleading expression, Travis decided it wouldn't hurt to answer a few questions about their mother. "Go ahead," Travis urged his daughter.

Matt's wife kissed his cheek, then joined the others in the kitchen. Samantha gazed into her husband, Wade's, eyes and Travis swore the couple shared an entire conversation without speaking a word. Wade hugged her, shot Travis a be-nice-to-my-wife glare and left.

"I'll make sure you're not disturbed," Duke said before vacating the hallway.

Travis nodded to the door Dominick had slammed moments earlier. "Maybe you should check on your father." *He's yours, too.* True, but for all intents and purposes, he and Dominick Cartwright were strangers who happened to look alike.

"This is unbelievable." Samantha cast a worried glance down the hallway.

"We could all use a drink," Matt said. They filed into the parlor and Travis positioned himself in front of the windows. His sister collapsed on the leather sofa and Matt poured scotch into three glasses at the wet bar. After serving the drinks, he sat in the chair near the fireplace.

Travis swirled the gold liquid in the crystal glass, thinking this was a three- or four-shot occasion—not a one-shot. He wasn't a conservative drinker, thanks to his chosen career. As soon as his two-week rotation on the rig ended and he stepped onto the mainland, Travis and his coworkers headed straight for the local bars to blow off steam. Even though he hadn't seen the harm in his bi-monthly binges, his mother had nagged him to cut back on his alcohol consumption. He hadn't appreciated her concern until she'd been diagnosed with cancer. After helping to raise Charlie, Travis owed his mother a lot more than a promise to watch his drinking. He would have done anything for his mom if it would have cured her illness.

Then she'd died and he'd discovered his whole life had been a lie. He'd grown up a latchkey kid, living in one-bedroom apartments because that's all his mom could afford on a secretary's salary. Only when he'd landed the job on his first rig had they been able to scrape together the down payment for a small house. He hadn't resented going without as a child—it was all he'd ever known. But the knowledge that he was the son of a wealthy oilman made him bitter.

"If you didn't look so much like our father," Matt said, "I'd accuse you of fabricating the story of Charlotte's death in order to blackmail Dad."

"I've lived thirty years without a dime of Cartwright oil money. No reason I can't go another thirty years without it." Travis sipped his scotch, savoring the burn of alcohol against his throat. Even though he understood his sibling's mistrust, he hated that he had to defend himself when he was the one who'd been wronged.

Samantha waved a hand in the air. "Enough talk about money. How did Charlotte die?"

"Cancer. Multiple myeloma," Travis said.

Matt tossed his drink back in one swallow. "What kind of cancer is that?"

"A tumor of the bone-marrow cells. Mom was diagnosed two years ago. After treatment she went into remission, which lasted nine months."

"When did she die?" Samantha wiped at a lone tear on her cheek.

Travis felt empathy for his sister, the emotion surprising him. He didn't know this woman, yet he couldn't deny their physical similarities and the weird connection he felt in his gut when they made eye contact.

"Mom passed away three weeks ago." Travis cursed the lump that formed in his throat. He was done crying for his mother. "I'm sorry." Not that the apology meant anything coming from a complete stranger.

"Did Charlotte ever talk about Matt and me?" Samantha asked.

"No." His answer startled Matt, and Travis regretted his bluntness.

"How did you find out about us?" Matt asked.

"Mom kept a diary." She'd mentioned leaving

Dominick and her two children—something poetic about heeding the call of her heart. All bullshit. When her remission ended, the entries had turned morose and she'd confessed that she'd regretted forsaking Matt and Samantha for a chance to be with her true love. Travis had yet to figure out just who the hell her true love had been. There had never been another man in his mother's life—at least not one that Travis had known about.

"Do you have Charlotte's diary with you?" Samantha asked.

"Yes." Maybe his sister and brother would find solace in her words. The diary had only pissed off Travis.

Matt shot out of the chair and paced in front of the fireplace. "I just remembered something." He stared at Travis. "This past summer Dad confessed that he should have gone after Charlotte when she'd walked out on us years ago. But he said his pride got in the way and he'd believed that she'd come to her senses and return on her own. Then months passed and there was no word from her, so Dad filed for divorce."

Feeling shaky, Travis left his post at the window and joined Samantha on the couch. What would his life have been like if his mother had had a change of heart and returned to the Lazy River? Or if Dominick had gone after her and convinced her to give their marriage another try?

"Did Dominick talk about our mother often?" Travis directed the question to Matt.

"Anytime Sam or I asked questions about her, Dad changed the subject." Matt glanced at Samantha. "Before Amy and I married, I considered hiring a private detective to find Charlotte."

"You did?" Samantha's expression softened.

Travis envied his siblings' close relationship. All these years he'd believed growing up an only child had been better than having to share a bedroom, clothes or toys with a brother or sister. He wasn't so sure now.

"I mentioned my plan to you, Sam, but you talked me out of it," Matt said.

"Really?" Samantha spoke her next words to Travis. "When I was a teenager, I had an accident—a horse kicked me in the head and I almost died." She smiled. "But I survived." The smile flipped upside down. "The bad thing is that my short-term memory was affected and I forget things."

"Amy encouraged me to invite Charlotte to our wedding," Matt said.

"Why did I talk you out of it?"

"You believed if Charlotte came to the wedding, she'd upset Dad. After giving it more thought, I decided you were right. Dad's always been there for us, and I didn't want to do anything that might hurt him."

"I felt the same," Travis said. "There was a time I toyed with the idea of searching for my father, but I never had the money to hire an investigator." And why bother if the man didn't want Travis in the first place?

"I don't understand how Dad couldn't have known about you all these years." The note of suspicion in Matt's voice didn't escape Travis.

"Poor Dad," Samantha said. "I'm worried about the toll the news of Charlotte's death will take on him."

Matt helped himself to more scotch. "He'll need time to get used to the idea that both his wives are now dead."

"Both wives?" Travis asked.

"Matt and I were teenagers when Dad married Duke's mother."

That explained Duke's presence in the family—a stepson.

"Laura died in a car accident several years ago," Matt said.

Travis's siblings had lost two mothers in their lifetime. "I'm sorry."

"The whole situation is sorry." Samantha stared into her drink.

"Did you bring proof of Charlotte's death?" Matt asked.

Yeah, her body's in the bed of my pickup. Travis squelched his anger. He couldn't find fault with his brother for wanting to protect his father. He'd have the same urge if this had happened to his mother. "I'll mail Dominick a copy of her death certificate as soon as Charlie and I return to Houston."

A peek at the wall clock told Travis that the three of them had been together a half hour and Dominick had yet to make an appearance. "It's best if Charlie and I leave." Having a civilized discussion about his mother's death was more than Travis could handle. "I'll leave my cell number in case Dominick changes his mind and wants to talk."

"Dad's going to want answers before you leave," Matt said. "You might as well stay here tonight so the two of you can talk tomorrow."

"The kids are planning to sleep in the bunkhouse. Charlie will love that. And this couch—" Samantha pointed to the piece of furniture she sat on "—is a sleeper sofa."

Okay, so they had room to put him and Charlie up

for the night, but the invitation wasn't heartfelt. Travis got the impression that Matt didn't trust him and wanted to keep an eye on him. "Charlie and I don't want to intrude."

"Thanksgiving is a time to be with family," Samantha said.

Family—the reason Travis and Charlie had embarked on the trip to Oklahoma in the first place. He couldn't return to Texas until Dominick agreed to care for Charlie should Travis suddenly drop out of the picture. And what about his daughter? Charlie hadn't smiled much or played with any friends since her grandmother's death.

"We'll stay."

"IF YOU'RE MY GRANDPA, how come you never visit me?"

Charlie's question met Travis's ear as he reached the bottom of the stairs. After tossing and turning on the sofa bed all night, he'd showered and changed in the second-floor bathroom and had been heading to breakfast.

"Who said I never wanted to visit you, Charlotte?"

"Why do you keep calling me Charlotte? My name's Charlie."

"Are you always this impudent?"

"Did you call me a swearword?"

The two needed a referee. Travis entered the kitchen. "Mornin'." He reached out to ruffle his daughter's hair, but she saw his hand coming and ducked. *Impudent* little stinker.

"Grandpa keeps calling me Grandma's name." His daughter thrust out her lower lip.

"Charlie prefers to be called Charlie," Travis said.

Dominick stood at the stove, flipping pancakes—avoiding eye contact. "Where is everyone?" Travis asked. The house was too quiet.

"Visiting Juanita's family."

"Grandpa said Juanita bosses him around."

Dominick set five miniature pancakes in front of Charlie, then slid the syrup bottle across the table. "Juanita's been my housekeeper since Char—for a long time."

The conversation baffled Travis. This was the first time his father had spoken directly to him since their arrival last night, and they were discussing the housekeeper. Dominick poured batter into the frying pan, his movements careful and precise. A couple of minutes later, he added a second plate of pancakes to the table and a large mug of coffee. "Dig in."

"Thanks." Travis reached for the syrup bottle.

"You're probably confused about who's related to whom in the family." Dominick refilled his coffee mug, then propped a hip against the kitchen counter.

Travis had a pretty good grasp on everyone's relationship, but kept quiet.

"Matt married Amy this past summer. She was a widow. Her daughters, Rose and Lily, are from her first marriage."

"Rose said that Lily pooped marbles all over the bathroom floor when Matt babysat them."

"We don't talk about stuff like that when we're eating," Travis said. Leave it to his daughter to add flavor to the morning meal.

"Amy owns a horse-boarding business in Idaho and

Matt raises cutting horses on her farm. I wish they lived closer. I don't get to see them often enough."

Travis steeled himself against the painful twinge caused by Dominick's words. Had Travis's mother not isolated him from the family, his father might have missed him, too.

"I married Duke's mother, Laura, when Duke was sixteen." Dominick stared into his coffee mug. "Laura passed away when Duke was in college."

"I'm sorry," Travis muttered. Why was he always muttering *sorry?* When would someone apologize to *him* for being cheated out of his rightful place in the Cartwright family?

"Is Grandpa sad?" Charlie whispered.

"Not anymore, Charlotte," Dominick answered.

Charlie opened her mouth to protest her proper name, but Travis nudged her hand and she settled for an eye roll.

"Duke transferred his information-and-technology company to Detroit a year ago. He met Renée there. She's a social worker. They adopted Timmy. Their baby's due in January."

Travis shoved a forkful of pancake into his mouth. He'd lost his appetite but felt obligated to eat, since Dominick had gone to the trouble of cooking for him.

"Samantha married Wade this past September. Wade opened his own investment firm and Samantha runs a rescue ranch for horses. Luke is Wade's son from his first marriage." Dominick joined Travis and Charlie at the table. "Do you have any brothers or sisters?" he asked Charlie.

"Nope. I don't even have a mom." Charlie shrugged. "My dad said she ran away after I was born."

Dominick's dark eyebrows arched. Travis made no excuses for being truthful with his daughter. He wished more than ever his own mother had been truthful with him.

"Is Julie ever gonna be my mom?" Charlie always referred to her mother by first name. Travis assumed it was only natural, since she didn't remember Julie.

"I don't know, Charlie."

"That's okay. At least I got a dad and you always come back when your job gets over." Charlie's smile zapped Travis's heart. He couldn't remember the last time his daughter had said something so nice to him.

"That's right, kiddo. I always come back."

"What kind of work do you do?" Dominick asked.

"My dad works on a big—" Charlie raised her arms above her head "—oil rig in the ocean."

For the first time since Travis had entered the kitchen, Dominick's expression lightened. "What rig?"

"Exxon Mobil Hoover Diana."

His father nodded as if he knew the exact location and history of the oil platform. "What's your position— rig manager?"

Yeah, sure. He needed a college degree to run an oil rig.

Travis didn't mention that he was up for a promotion following his leave of absence from the rig. After a few false starts with his career, he'd begun taking his job seriously. His dedication had paid off. The rig manager had rewarded his strong work ethic by assigning tasks outside a roughneck's general duties. Travis had learned more about operating a rig in the past two years than he had in all his years working for oil companies. "I'm a roughneck."

The light fizzled from Dominick's eyes. "Everyone has to work their way up the ladder."

Travis's gut tightened. He shouldn't care if Dominick was disappointed that his long-lost son was a lowly deckhand. What had the old man expected when Travis had been raised by a single mother who'd barely managed to make ends meet? Unlike Matt, Samantha and Duke, Travis hadn't lived a privileged life.

"How long have you worked on rigs?" Dominick asked.

"Nine years."

His father's eyes rounded.

Travis had been young and rebellious his first few years in the business. He'd been put on probation twice and fired once. Like a lot of young hotheads without male role models in their lives, it had taken longer for Travis to settle down.

"So your grandmother took care of you while your dad worked?" Dominick's voice shook when he asked Charlie the question. Travis wondered if the emotion was fueled by anger or sadness.

"Grandma was the best, but she's in heaven now. She's one of God's angels." Charlie tugged Travis's shirtsleeve. "Can I go visit Fred?"

"Who's Fred?"

"Grandpa's old dog. He slept with us in the bunkhouse. He's got 'thritus, right, Grandpa?"

"Arthritis," Dominick clarified, then fired off another question at his granddaughter. "How old are you?"

"Eight. I'm in second grade and my birthday's March 25th."

"You're awfully small for an eight-year-old. Do you drink enough milk?"

"I don't know. Do I, Dad?" Charlie asked.

"Plenty." Then Travis added for his father's benefit, "Charlie's mother is a petite woman."

"What's *petite?*" Charlie asked.

"Little, like you," Travis answered.

"Julie's really pretty. Dad's got lots of pictures of her."

Lots equated to a half-dozen snapshots he'd taken of Julie when they'd first begun dating. He'd kept the photos for Charlie's sake—and to remind himself that pretty blondes were a waste of time.

"Brush your teeth before you play with the dog," Travis said. A few weeks ago, he'd caught Charlie licking a dab of paste from the tube instead of using her toothbrush. Now he checked the bristles to make sure they were wet. She'd yet to figure out how he knew when she hadn't brushed her teeth.

"I'll brush 'em later."

"Now." He and his daughter engaged in a staredown. After several seconds, Charlie stomped out of the room.

"Spirited young gal," Dominick said.

"I'd like to speak with you in private about Charlie before we leave."

"You're leaving?"

Had Dominick forgotten his rude behavior the previous night when he'd slammed his office door in Travis's face? "It's obvious you don't want us here." No sense beating around the bush.

"I don't like surprises."

Travis caught a glimpse of fear in his father's eyes. What did the old man have to be afraid of?

"I'd like you and Charlotte to spend Thanksgiving with the family."

Travis wasn't used to being around a big family. Samantha seemed nice enough, but Matt and Duke had kept their distance the previous night. He'd rather settle his business with Dominick and leave.

Before Travis found a way to turn down the invitation, Dominick asked, "Do you have other plans for the holiday?"

"No."

"Then it's settled. You and Charlotte will stay here." Dominick set his coffee cup in the sink, then lifted his coat from a hook by the back door. "Tell Charlotte I'll be in the barn, waiting for her."

As Travis gathered the dirty dishes, he didn't know whether to be relieved or worried that Dominick had insisted he and Charlie remain at the Lazy River awhile longer. He wanted to learn what had gone wrong between his parents, but feared his mother would be made out to be the villain.

Charlie raced into the kitchen, shoving her arms into her jacket sleeves. "Where's Grandpa?"

"Waiting for you in the barn."

His daughter dashed outside.

A knock sounded at the door just as Travis had finished loading the dishwasher. The schoolteacher stood on the porch. Her eyes widened when their gazes connected.

"I can't believe I didn't notice the resemblance before now."

Travis had better get used to that reaction if he intended to stick around the area. "C'mon in." She stepped into the kitchen and he closed the door against the cold.

She was taller than he'd first guessed, standing only a few inches shorter than his own six-foot-two-inch height.

"Sara Sanders." She held out her hand.

"Travis Cartwright." He grasped her fingers, surprised when he felt calluses on her palm—not the hands of a typical schoolteacher. "My daughter's name is Charlie."

A hint of a smile toyed with Sara's mouth. "Ah, yes, the little walrus."

"I don't know where she got the idea to stick straws up her nose." Travis caught the clean scent that wafted in the air around Sara's head. Soap. Not perfume. He looked out the kitchen window and spotted a white compact parked next to his truck. Sara drove an economical, no-frills vehicle.

"The resemblance is uncanny," she said, staring at his face.

"Dominick is my father."

"My family's ranch borders the Lazy River and we've never heard of a fourth Cartwright sibling."

"Dominick had no idea I existed."

"Amazing."

"Coffee?"

"No, thanks." Sara's attention shifted to the doorway.

"Dominick's in the barn with Charlie."

"Where are the rest of the Cartwrights?"

"Visiting the housekeeper."

Up close, Sara was definitely a plain Jane. Tall. Serious. Tiny crow's-feet fanned from the corner of her eyes, insisting she spent as many days in the sun as she did in the classroom. He guessed her age to be around his own. "Are you and Dominick *friends?*" He emphasized the word *friend,* suspecting women of all ages pursued Dominick...or rather his millions.

"Hardly. We're not even friendly neighbors." She motioned out the window. "Do you know how long he'll be?"

Travis shrugged. "You're welcome to go out and speak with him if you want."

"I guess I'll take that cup of coffee and wait." She draped her coat over the back of the chair.

Considering that most of his days and nights were spent in the company of rabble-rousers, when Travis was with a woman the last thing he cared to do was talk. "Where do you teach?" He set two mugs on the table and joined Sara.

"Tulapoint Elementary. The school serves the ranching community in our area." She sipped her coffee. "What do you do for a living?"

"I work on oil rigs."

"I imagine Dominick appreciates having one son who loves oil as much as he does."

The verdict was still out. Before Travis had a chance to pry information about his father out of Sara, the front door crashed open.

Charlie's shoes slapped against the wood floor. "Dad! Grandpa says we can take Fred home with us if we want him." She skidded to a halt in the kitchen doorway. "You're the lady from that pink house my dad and I ate in."

Dominick joined Charlie in the kitchen. When he noticed his neighbor, the smile on his face evaporated. "Sara."

"Sara would like to speak with you." Travis stood. "C'mon, Charlie, let's check on—"

"Stay."

Travis froze.

"Have you decided to sell to me?" Dominick asked Sara.

Sara's broad shoulders stiffened. "Is there somewhere we can talk in private?"

"Charlie, go upstairs and brush your teeth," Travis said.

"I already did."

"Then brush them again."

"Jeez," Charlie muttered beneath her breath and stomped from the room.

Sara pulled a letter from the pocket of her coat and thrust it at Dominick. "What's the meaning of this?"

"Self-explanatory, isn't it?"

"You intend to sue us for damages?"

Sue? Travis gaped at his father.

"I didn't say much when one or two of your cows got loose on my land, but the whole herd broke through your fence last week and grazed my property."

"I'm sure the fifty head of cattle you keep for show didn't miss the three acres of grass our cows consumed before Cole and Gabe herded them back to the Bar T."

"That's not the point." Dominick rubbed his jaw. "You Sanders are in over your heads."

"We're not selling the Bar T."

"Your brothers feel differently about the situation."

"I'm keeping my promise to my father—I'm not handing over our ranch to a greedy old man who already owns half the state of Oklahoma."

"Then you'd better hire yourself a good lawyer."

Sara's chin jutted.

"Travis, talk some sense into my neighbor." Dominick left the room.

"Well?" Sara huffed.

Travis blinked. "Well, what?"

"How do you plan to persuade me to give in to your father?"

"I don't."

"Why not? I thought all you Cartwright's stuck together?"

"This is your fight, not mine. I'm heading back to Houston in a few days."

Was it Travis's imagination or had the fire in Sara Sanders' eyes banked at his pronouncement?

Chapter Three

"Is it true that some guy showed up at the Lazy River, claiming to be a Cartwright?" Sara's eldest brother, Cole, asked when she entered the barn Thanksgiving morning.

Tulapoint wasn't a town, rather a map dot boasting a population of 323 people. It took only one phone call to crank the engine on the rumor mill. Not even a national holiday quieted the gossipmongers.

"'Fraid so." Sara had been shocked that the man she'd seen at Beulah's two evenings ago had been a Cartwright—according to rumors, a son Dominick had never known existed. "Wilma phoned earlier and said Samantha brought her a pumpkin pie." The retired Sunday-school instructor battled lupus and, since she'd never married or had children, the local women checked in on her.

"What else did Samantha tell Wilma about the guy?"

"Travis broke the news that their mother recently died of cancer." No matter the strain between the Sanderses and the Cartwrights, Sara felt sorry for Samantha and Matt. She suspected they'd held out hope that one day they might be reunited with their mother.

Cole grabbed a curry comb from the grooming belt around his hips and brushed Son of Sunshine's coat. Her brother had purchased the infamous American quarter horse from Matt Cartwright for a measly five-hundred bucks. Their neighbor hadn't said how he'd come to own the sterile stud and Cole hadn't asked. SOS possessed a keen intelligence and plenty of "cow" attitude and heart. Pair those qualities with the animal's ability to perform pinpoint stops, starts and turns, and Cole believed he'd landed the deal of the century.

"I doubt Dominick was too torn up over Charlotte's death," her brother said.

"According to Wilma, Travis and his daughter have been living in Houston with Charlotte all these years."

"Is Travis married?"

"I don't know." Sara hadn't noticed a wedding band, but that didn't mean anything. Regardless of his marital status, she doubted a man as good looking as Travis suffered from a lack of female attention. Not that she cared about his love life. Sara was so over men, it wasn't even funny.

Like most women her age, she wanted to marry and start a family of her own, but the one man she'd set her heart on had taught her a painful lesson—handsome men weren't interested in country girls unless they had an ulterior motive. Her father had hired Josh as an extra hand during branding season and it didn't take the cowboy long to cozy up to Sara and propose to her.

Once she'd fallen under Josh's spell, he'd run off in the middle of the night with the Bar T's prized bull, Sweetwater Blackie, in tow. The authorities had never been able to track down the bull and suspected Josh had sold the animal on the black market to a rancher somewhere in Mexico. Not only had Josh broken Sara's heart, he'd stolen a fifteen-thousand-dollar bull and had made a fool out of her in front of family and friends.

After tucking the comb into the grooming belt, Cole led SOS outside and turned him loose in the paddock. Sara followed, planting her boot on the bottom rail. She stared into the distance for as far as the eye could see. Winter had turned the once lush green valley a dull, golden brown. Off in the distance, gently rolling hills were dotted with leafless oak and cypress trees. Sara loved this land. Come spring the area would transform into a verdant paradise as Black Angus grazed the green valleys, creating a picturesque setting.

I'm running out of options, Daddy. Help me find a way to save the ranch.

"Did Travis know about Dominick all these years?"

"No. Samantha told Wilma that Travis discovered his mother's diary after Charlotte died and that's when he learned Dominick was his father."

"And Dominick didn't know Charlotte was pregnant with Travis when she left him?"

"Obviously not or Dominick would have demanded custody of Travis, too, don't you think?" Dominick's wealth and standing in Oklahoma's oil industry allowed him to do anything he wanted—like harass his neighbors and threaten his competitors until they were forced to lowball their leasing bids for the Bar T. No matter, she refused to negotiate a business deal with Dominick.

Sara wished she could skim Charlotte's journal.

During the final days of her father's battle with pulmonary fibrosis, he'd drifted in and out of consciousness. Right before the end, he'd called out for Charlotte. For as far back as Sara could remember, neither of her parents had ever spoken the woman's name or discussed her whereabouts.

"What does Travis do for a living?" Cole asked.

"He's a roughneck."

"The oil baron finally got his wish—a son in the oil business."

Whether Travis lived and breathed black crude as Dominick did was anybody's guess. Both men worked in the petroleum industry, but Travis's shocked expression when Dominick had threatened her hinted that he might not possess his father's cutthroat business acumen.

Two years ago, her father had been forced to take out a second mortgage on the Bar T after the cattle ranch had suffered financial losses from drought and disease. Afraid they'd lose the ranch, Cole had coaxed their father into commissioning a geological survey of the property. If the soil tests were positive for oil, then their father would lease the drilling rights and use the income to pay off the bank, invest in a new bull for the herd and make needed repairs to the property.

As soon as their father received the good news that there was oil beneath the Bar T, he sought leasing bids, but the oil companies lowballed their bids. Then Dominick had asked to buy the Bar T and Sara's father had been certain that Dominick had manipulated his competitors. Furious, her father had sworn he'd die before Dominick Cartwright ever got his hands on the

Bar T. Three months later, her father's health took a turn for the worse and the ranch went further in debt as the medical bills piled up.

Unless Dominick dropped the bogus lawsuit and stopped influencing the other oil companies, there was no way Sara could prevent the bank from taking the ranch. She needed a miracle. Christmas was right around the corner—maybe Santa would stuff her stocking with a hundred thousand dollars. Ho. Ho. Ho.

"Turkey almost done?" Cole nudged her side, interrupting Sara's musings.

"In about an hour."

Sara lived in an old Victorian near the elementary school in town. After her mother had passed away, she'd made the trek out to the Bar T each Thanksgiving and Christmas to prepare a holiday meal for her father and brothers. When her father had died this past April, she'd decided to continue the tradition until she or one of her brothers married.

Right now the odds of any of them tying the knot were slim-to-none. Gabe was a notorious one-night-stand cowboy and the ranch kept Cole too busy to date, which left Sara. After being burned by love once, she was done with cowboys and ranchers—in this neck of the woods that meant slim pickings for husbands.

"Where's Gabe?"

"Sleeping." Cole snorted. "He stumbled in at three this morning."

Gabe went through women faster than a seasoned cowboy ate cold beans.

"Need help in the barn?" Sara had chosen a teaching career, but she'd grown up punching cows alongside her brothers. With her height and sturdy build, there weren't many ranch chores she couldn't handle.

"Leave the mucking to Gabe. A little fresh air and manure ought to cure his hangover." Cole walked off and Sara returned to the house.

Memories of Sara's father kept her company while she put the finishing touches on the meal. She'd been daddy's little girl—or rather, tomboy. Much to her mother's dismay, Sara had been her father's constant shadow around the ranch. In his final months of life when he'd been hooked up to an oxygen tank, struggling to breathe, he'd made Sara swear not to allow Cole or Gabe to talk her into selling out to Dominick. Easier said than done.

Sara removed the turkey from the oven and delivered it to the dining-room table, then clanged the supper bell on the back porch. A few minutes later, Cole walked through the door and Gabe stumbled from his bedroom—hair matted to his head and wearing the previous night's clothes.

"Smells good." Gabe yawned.

"You need a shower." Sara placed a bowl of mashed potatoes next to the meat platter.

Ignoring her comment, Gabe took a seat, then reached for a turkey leg. Sara slapped his wrist. "Touch it and you die." She made two more trips into the kitchen before sitting across from Cole. "We're saying Grace." She clasped her brothers' hands and bowed her head. "Dear Lord, thank You for blessing us with this meal. I'm grateful for my brothers and ask that You keep them safe from harm." She opened one eye and peered at Gabe. "What are you thankful for?"

"Thank You, God, for introducing me to Wynona last night. She's one hot chili pepper."

Sara kicked his shin.

"Ouch!" Gabe winced.

"Your turn." She stared at Cole.

"Thank You for my sister, who cooked this fine meal. Amen." Cole reached for the meat platter.

No use conversing until her brothers appeased their hunger. They tore into the food like vultures, scraping the bowls clean—so much for leftovers. Before she dished up the pumpkin pie she broached her least-favorite topic—their neighbor. "Dominick won't drop the lawsuit."

"Figured he wouldn't," Cole said. "He wants our oil but he doesn't want to pay us what it's worth."

Gabe slouched in his chair, rubbing his belly as he stared into space—probably dreaming about the hot chili pepper.

"Be right back." Sara retrieved the pumpkin pie and whipped cream from the kitchen and returned to the dining room. She'd never told her brothers about their father's final shout out to Charlotte Cartwright on his deathbed. Now that Travis had made himself known, she wondered if there was more to her father and Charlotte's relationship than being neighbors. While her brothers finished dessert, Sara pondered. Was Dominick simply a greedy businessman or did he have a personal vendetta against her father? Whatever had caused the rift between the two men should have been laid to rest along with her father when he'd died.

"Don't mean to change the subject—" Gabe pushed his plate away "—but since we're all together, I might as well spill the news."

Alarm bells went off in Sara's head. "What news?"

"I'm leaving."

"Where to?" Cole asked.

"Out on the road with a few buddies." He waggled his eyebrows. "Might try rodeoing."

"What about money for entry fees?" Cole glared across the table.

"I've got some saved." Gabe shrugged. "If I run low, I'll pick up work as a ranch hand somewhere."

Sara flung her napkin at her brother's face. "You'll work for another ranch but you won't lift a finger to help your own family?"

"I might if I knew this place would belong to us forever. It's only a matter of time before we lose the ranch," he said. "I know you promised Dad you'd do everything in your power to keep from selling, but even Dad would recognize when to cut his losses. You can't best Dominick. Besides, his bid was generous and—"

"Generous? Dominick's a crook," Sara protested.

"If you don't negotiate with him, the bank will take the ranch, then turn around and sell it to Dominick anyway. And we'll walk away with nothing."

Gabe made a valid point, but Sara wasn't ready to raise the white flag.

"I'm taking off in the morning." Her brother shoved his chair back and stood.

Sara poked Cole's shoulder. "Say something."

"What do you want me to say? 'Stay, Gabe? Stay and work your ass off for nothing?'"

Tears clogged Sara's throat. "But Dad—"

"Dad's dead, and we can't hold off the creditors forever. If we lose the ranch, which is the road we're headed down now, you'll have your house in town and

Gabe and I will have nothing but our trucks and the clothes on our backs."

"I promised Dad that Dominick would never get his hands on this ranch."

"You made that promise, Sara." Gabe pointed to Cole, then himself. "We didn't."

Cole got up from the table. "Thanks for making dinner."

"Yeah, sure," she whispered. Some Thanksgiving this turned out to be.

Chaos.

Thanksgiving in the Cartwright household was unlike anything Travis or his daughter had ever experienced. Bodies everywhere. Kids shouting and racing from room to room. Good-natured arguing. And laughter. Plenty of laughter.

Travis stood in the family room, pretending interest in the football game on TV while covertly observing his siblings and their families. The past two days, he'd felt as if he'd been riding an emotional roller-coaster with no off switch. His mother's death hadn't sunk in, yet he found himself surrounded by family he hadn't known existed until a few weeks ago.

"Having second thoughts?" Duke stopped at his side.

"About what?" Travis studied his stepbrother's outfit—Western dress shirt with pearl snaps, bolo tie, Texas-size belt buckle and snakeskin boots. Obviously the Detroit executive loved dressing the part of a cowboy.

"Second thoughts about being a Cartwright." Duke

glanced across the room, his expression softening when he saw his wife. "Dominick can be overwhelming."

"And evasive," Travis said. "I've asked to speak to him in private, but he's avoiding me."

"Maybe he doesn't trust you."

Travis understood his siblings' doubts about him, but shouldn't his father feel differently? "Trust me how?"

Duke narrowed his eyes. "Maybe Dominick assumes all you care about is getting your hands on his oil money."

"I don't give a crap about his wealth."

"If that's true, I don't know whether to admire you or pity you."

"I get that you're protective of Matt and Samantha, but—"

"Matt and Sam had a rough childhood growing up without a mother. Even though they're adults, they've yearned for a mother's love their entire lives, which makes them vulnerable to you."

What about him? He'd yearned for a father's love all his life.

"You're their only connection to Charlotte." Duke stepped in front of Travis, blocking his view of the family. "Don't even think about taking advantage of Matt, Sam or Dominick. You mess with my family and you mess with me. Got it?"

Yeah, Travis got it, all right. No matter that he was Dominick's biological son, he was still an outsider. "Message received."

Duke's posture relaxed when he changed the subject. "Renée said Charlie's mom isn't in the picture anymore."

Evidently Charlie had spilled the beans about their

life in Houston. Travis didn't care. He had no secrets. "Julie left after Charlie was born." Travis didn't go into details. No matter how he told the story of Julie abandoning him and a baby, he always came out looking like an idiot.

"Renée's seen everything in her job as a social worker. She says Charlie's a well-adjusted little girl for having grown up without a mother."

"Her grandmother gets credit for that." Travis worried about the impact his mother's death would have on Charlie in the long run. He wasn't opposed to marriage, but his job on the rig made relationships stressful. Travis would hate to marry and then have Charlie become attached to the woman only to be abandoned again when the stress of his work schedule caused another woman to pack her bags and leave.

"You like rig work?" Duke asked.

Travis studied his stepbrother, unsure if he was making polite conversation or was genuinely interested in Travis's answer.

"Don't get me wrong—I love my job." Duke shrugged. "But every day is the same. Meetings. Phone calls. Emails."

Oil rig work was exhausting, but Travis preferred physical labor over a desk job. "The crew on the rig is like a second family. We celebrate and argue like brothers, uncles." *Fathers.* "At the end of a two-week rotation, I'm more than ready to return to the mainland."

"Mind if I join the conversation?" Matt motioned to Travis's almost empty beer bottle. "Need another one?"

"No, I'm good."

"Did you thank him?" Matt asked Duke.

"Not yet. We were discussing other matters." Duke sent a warning smile Travis's way.

"We'd like to thank you," Matt said.

"For what?"

"For choosing a career in oil."

Roughnecking wasn't a career so much as a job.

"Dad's been holding out hope that Duke or I would change our minds and work for Cartwright Oil." Matt chuckled. "I'd rather shovel horse manure than dig oil wells and Mr. Corporate here would rather brainstorm information systems than analyze oil productivity spreadsheets."

Travis directed his words to Matt. "Our mother was the one who pushed me to sign up with a rig."

"Your days of roughnecking will soon be over." Matt and Duke exchanged a silent message. "When you turn thirty-two, you'll have access to your trust fund."

Trust fund? "I didn't come here for a handout."

"No matter," Matt said. "You'll get your share of Cartwright money just like the rest of us."

No one could force him to accept his inheritance, but if what his brothers claimed was true, then Travis had to consider Charlie. He wanted to make sure she was provided for if something happened to him. Still…he hated that his siblings assumed he intended to sponge off their father.

"What are you guys discussing?" Samantha joined the group. "Why the serious faces?"

Ignoring their sister's question, Matt nodded toward the front door. "Where's Wade taking the kids?"

"To the bunkhouse to teach them how to rope the fake steer Dad bought a few weeks ago."

"C'mon." Duke nudged Matt in the side. "Wade couldn't throw a rope if his life depended on it."

"Be nice," Samantha scolded.

"Don't worry, sis. We won't hurt your hubby's feelings." Chuckling, Matt followed Duke outside.

Relieved to be rid of his brothers and their suspicions, Travis turned his attention to his sister. Her eyes were the same shape and brown color of his. He and Samantha looked more like brother and sister than she and Matt.

"I read Charlotte's diary last night." Her sad smile reminded Travis that he hadn't been the only one hurt by his mother's actions.

"Did it help you remember her?" he asked.

"Not really. I was two when she left. Matt was four. He claims he doesn't have any memories of Charlotte, but I think he has a few."

Travis had grown up with a mother's love. Samantha and Matt had grown up with a father's love. On that score they were even. But Dominick was still alive and that gave Travis the advantage of forging a relationship with his estranged father—if he cared to. His siblings would never have that opportunity with their mother.

"I think Charlotte missed me and Matt. That's something, I guess." The wobble in her voice sucker punched Travis in the gut.

"I'm sorry, Samantha."

"You'd better stop calling me Samantha. Everyone in the family calls me Sam."

"How come you're not suspicious of me like the others?" His sister was the only person in the house who didn't act uncomfortable around him.

She squeezed his arm. "A close call with death makes

a person look at life in a different light. Each day I have with my family is a gift. I don't view you and Charlie as a threat—I see you as a blessing."

Travis appreciated his sister's acceptance. "Mom wasn't a mean person. I don't know why she walked out on you and Matt and kept me from the rest of the family."

His comment brought tears to his sister's eyes. "Have you had a chance to speak privately with Dad?"

Dad. The word sounded foreign in Travis's ear. "No."

"He's hiding out in his office right now."

So that's where the old man had holed up. Time was running out. Travis had one week left of his leave of absence from the rig and he'd yet to make child-care arrangements for Charlie. Tomorrow he intended to return to Houston to begin searching for a nanny.

"Dad can be a grouch, but give him the benefit of the doubt. He's a good man." She caught Travis by surprise and hugged him, then left the room.

The door to Dominick's office stood partially open.

"Come in."

When Travis entered the room, the first thing he noticed was the massive mahogany desk taking up half the space. The football game played on the flat-screen TV mounted on the wall across from the desk and bookcases filled the back of the room. Various antique oil artifacts occupied the shelves along with family photos.

"Have a seat." Dominick kept his eyes on the documents in front of him.

Travis closed the door, then sank onto the leather couch. "If you're busy—"

"I'm always busy. Oil never stops flowing." Dominick tossed his reading glasses onto the desk blotter. "Why did you take a job on an oil rig?"

"Ran out of options. I'd gotten in trouble with the law." At his father's raised eyebrow, Travis explained. "Disorderly conduct charge and two drunk-driving tickets. Mom said I needed to find a better way to blow off steam. She suggested—" more like threatened "—that I apply for a job with one of the oil companies."

"Charlotte told you to work on a rig?"

"You sound surprised."

Dominick shrugged.

"Mind if I ask what happened between you and my mother?"

"As a matter of fact, I do mind." He stroked his mustache, then asked, "Did your mother ever remarry?"

"No. She worked as a secretary at a car dealership until Charlie came along, then she quit her job to stay home and take care of her when I worked on the rig."

"And you supported both Charlotte and Charlie?"

"I make decent money on the rig." Travis and his mother hadn't lived extravagantly, but between his paycheck and his mother's small retirement from her job at the dealership they'd managed to make ends meet.

"I could have given you both a hell of a lot more."

When Travis reflected on his mother's life, he acknowledged her day-to-day existence hadn't been exciting. No secret lovers. No high-society social events. No exotic travel or beautiful vacation home. Not even a brand-new car. What had caused his mother to trade in a life of luxury for a make-ends-meet existence?

"I'd like to discuss Charlie," Travis said.

Dominick grinned. "She's a pistol."

Travis wasn't sure if that was a compliment or not. He loved his daughter but the past couple of years had been tough on her. Travis and his mother had become lax in the discipline department. "She's a little rough around the edges."

"Like her father?"

Touché. "Now that Mom's gone and Charlie's mother isn't in the picture…" He hated talking about death, but in his line of work, dying on the job was a real possibility. After the Deepwater Horizon disaster, Travis's mother had convinced him to make out a will and he'd granted full custody of Charlie to his mother should he die. "I'm concerned that if something happens to me on the rig, there won't be anyone to take care of Charlie. I was hoping you'd consider—"

"You're asking me if I'd take in my grand-daughter?"

"Yes."

"In a heartbeat," Dominick said, his voice hoarse.

Travis hadn't meant to offend the old man, but he was relieved his daughter wouldn't be left in the state's care if he kicked the bucket before she reached eighteen. "As soon as we return to Houston, I'll have a new will drawn up."

"What will you do with Charlie when you're working on the rig?"

"I'm hoping to hire a live-in nanny."

"That can be expensive."

"We'll manage."

"Do you like your job?" Dominick asked.

"The past few months I've been shadowing a

motorhand and learning how to maintain the drilling rig engines, transmissions, hydraulic systems and electric generators." Travis was good with tools and a quick study. He hoped his supervisor would follow through with his promise of a promotion to rig technician if Travis passed all the mechanical exams.

"How much money are you making?" Dominick had been in the oil business his entire life. He knew roughnecks were the low men on the totem pole. "Fifty thousand?"

"Forty-five."

"Would you consider a position with Cartwright Oil for triple your current salary?"

A job that earned over a hundred thousand dollars a year?

"After taxes," Dominick added.

Shit. That was a lot of money. "What kind of job?"

"Rig technician. I could use another man in the field to help maintain the equipment on my rigs in Oklahoma and Arkansas."

"Don't you have several employees in that job right now?"

"You can never have enough experienced men in the field. Equipment breakdowns can cost hundreds of thousands of dollars a week in lost profits."

Dominick's confidence in him pleased Travis, but he doubted the workers on the rigs would accept him as easily. He'd have to work his butt off to prove he deserved the job. *You'd have a chance to show your father what you're made of.*

"You're a natural fit for the job," Dominick said. "If you decide to take me up on the offer, I could use your help with something else."

"What's that?"

"You and Sara Sanders are both single and around the same age—"

"I'm not interested in—"

"Of course you're not attracted to a woman like her, but I'm sure you could gain her trust and convince her to sell the Bar T to me."

Sara Sanders's face popped into Travis's mind. He admired her stubborn determination and refusal to allow his father to intimidate her, but he doubted she could hold out forever against Dominick. It was only a matter of time before Cartwright Oil won. Still… "You want me to bully her into doing business with you?"

"I never said you should threaten her." Dominick shrugged. "She's a single woman with few prospects. Give her some of your time and attention and before you know it, she'll be signing on the dotted line."

Travis had never led a woman on before and didn't care to begin now, but his father was handing him an opportunity to win his favor. Travis was eager to fit in with his new family and prove to his siblings that he had no ulterior motive where the Cartwright fortune was concerned. What could it hurt to become friends with Sara Sanders? If he convinced her to sell to Dominick, all the better.

"What kind of housing is available in the area?" Travis asked.

"You're welcome to stay on the ranch with me. There's plenty of room in the house for the three of us now that Samantha and Wade have moved into their new home. I'm away on business several days a week, so you and Charlie would have the place to yourselves most of the time." Dominick snapped his fingers. "Juanita's kids are grown. She'd be willing to stay overnight or keep Charlie with her at her place if we're both on the road at the same time."

"What about Matt and Samantha? Shouldn't you discuss this with them?" He didn't want Matt accusing him of mooching off their father.

"I've never asked for my children's approval before and I won't start now."

Travis wasn't all that bothered by his siblings' lukewarm reception. They had every right to be protective of their father. Travis would have felt the same way about his mother if Matt and Samantha had shown up unannounced on their doorstep. Travis was more concerned with Charlie and how she'd adjust. Overwhelmed by the turn of events, Travis said, "I'll think it over."

"What's to think over? I'm giving you a chance of a lifetime."

Dominick shuffled papers and straightened items on his desk—all businesslike—but Travis sensed a vulnerability in the old man he hadn't noticed before. If he wasn't mistaken, he swore the job offer was Dominick's way of trying to make up for years of not being there for Travis.

Father-son relationship aside, Travis was dying to prove that he was more than a roughneck. That he was capable of handling the job at Cartwright Oil.

Don't forget Charlie.

Relocating to the Lazy River would allow his daughter a chance to be part of a larger family, which would help her cope with the grief of losing her grandmother. Christmas was right around the corner and he and Charlie wouldn't have to celebrate alone. Besides, working for Dominick would enable them to spend more time together.

And there was Sara. If he could sway her to negotiate a business deal with Dominick, he'd earn a few brownie points. No one had ever accused Travis of turning down a challenge. "I'll give you an answer soon." He got up from the couch.

"I understand learning about me after all these years is a shock, but I have a lot of questions about your relationship with my mother." Travis opened the door, then paused. "Don't assume those questions will go away if I decide to work for you." He shut the door before Dominick had a chance to respond.

Chapter Four

"How come I'm gonna go to school here?" Charlie asked as Travis drove into Tulapoint Monday morning to register her for school.

The Cartwright siblings and their families had departed the Lazy River Ranch yesterday afternoon, leaving Travis plenty of time to consider Dominick's offer to work for him. When Travis woke this morning, he'd phoned the rig manager on the Hoover Diana. After explaining the situation to his boss, Travis had been assured that if things didn't work out in Oklahoma, he'd have a job waiting for him back in Houston.

With his boss's blessing, Travis decided to take the position at Cartwright Oil. He eagerly awaited the opportunity to show his father that, although he was a lowly roughneck, he possessed his fair share of business acumen. He decided the best way to demonstrate his talents was to persuade Sara Sanders to sell the Bar T to Dominick.

"Your grandfather wants us to move to the Lazy River." Travis broke the news to his daughter. "I'm going to work for his company."

"Grandpa's got a rig in the ocean?"

Charlie's quick acceptance of Dominick as her

grandfather amazed Travis, because he still struggled to make the connection between the word *dad* and Dominick. "Your grandfather's rigs are on land in Oklahoma and Arkansas."

"Where's Arkansas?"

"That way." Travis pointed east out the windshield. "I'll be checking the wells and helping to fix problems that crop up." He had never held a job where he told others what to do—he'd always been the one taking orders. He hadn't a clue how his father's employees would react to him, but he planned to earn their respect the old-fashioned way—by rolling up his sleeves and jumping in to help when needed.

"Are you excited about going to a new school?" he asked, changing the subject.

"No." Charlie crossed her arms over her chest. "The kids are gonna be mean."

That she was more concerned with her classmates than leaving behind a best friend in Houston proved his daughter had sacrificed a lot while her grandmother had battled cancer. When his mother had become housebound, Charlie's friends had fallen by the wayside. Hopefully a new school would provide her with a fresh start in the friendship department.

"Figure out who the nice kids are and hang around them," he said.

"They're gonna make fun of my name."

"Go by Charlotte, if you want."

She ignored his suggestion and asked, "What's gonna happen to all my toys and books and—"

"After you're settled in school today, I'm heading to Houston to pack our things."

"Who's gonna take care of me when you go to the rigs?"

"Your grandfather or Juanita." Charlie had met the housekeeper when the older woman had stopped at the ranch to say goodbye to Travis's siblings and their families.

"Who's gonna take me to school?"

"Dominick said the school bus will pick you up at the end of his driveway."

Charlie's mouth dropped open. "I gotta walk all that way to the bus?"

"If I'm not around, then Juanita or Grandpa will drive you in the car and wait with you until the bus arrives."

Right now Travis wished for the *old* Charlie back— the one who pouted and refused to speak. He could use a break from all the questions. The truck zipped past Beulah's pink Victorian and a mile later he noticed the sign for Tulapoint. He eased his foot off the accelerator and dropped the truck's speed to twenty-five miles per hour.

Downtown Tulapoint consisted of a handful of weathered brick and clapboard businesses. Mama's Café advertised a ninety-nine-cent breakfast burrito and an all-you-can-eat BBQ buffet on Mondays. An old two-story home had been converted into a business called Tina's Trinkets & Tea House. A white travel trailer with a giant blue snow cone on the roof sat in the parking lot of Gunderson's Drugstore. *Closed for the Season* had been spray-painted across the boarded up windows. Bank of Oklahoma and Kendall Hardware & Tack occupied one city block. Across from the bank a neon Michelob sign advertised Casey's Bar & Grill.

Travis slowed the truck to a crawl as he drove through a school zone.

"This place sucks."

"I thought Grandma told you not to say that word," Travis scolded.

"Grandma's not here anymore." Charlie's lower lip wobbled and Travis cursed his insensitivity.

His mother's death didn't feel real. He'd hardly mourned for her before he'd discovered the diary and all hell had broken loose. Charlie was too young to wonder why they'd never had any contact with the rest of their family, but it was only a matter of time before she asked. He hoped by then he'd have the answers.

"There's the school."

"Where?"

"Up ahead." The one-story brick building appeared well maintained. As he pulled into the parking lot, he noticed a handful of older homes behind the elementary school. Railroad tracks ran parallel to the houses and a rusty grain elevator sat empty at the abandoned station.

"It's puny," Charlie said.

His daughter's school in Houston housed pre-K through fifth grades with four classes in each grade. This school would be lucky to have one class for each grade. "Small can be a good thing.

"The playground's nice," he added. A chain-link fence enclosed the school yard, which consisted of swings, climbing apparatus and plenty of asphalt for playing dodge ball, jump rope and four square.

"Dad?"

"Yeah."

"If we live with Grandpa, does that mean you and me get to spend more time together?"

Travis sucked in a quiet breath. He'd always believed he'd been a decent parent—unlike Julie, he hadn't run from the responsibility of raising their child. He'd kept a roof over Charlie's head and food on the table. He'd paid for her clothing and medical care, but he'd done it from a distance. His mother's death had opened his eyes to what he really was—an absentee father. *Just like Dominick had been for Travis.*

"I promise we'll do more things together when I get back from Houston. And—" he tweaked Charlie's nose "—now that I'm working for Grandpa, I'll be able to come to your concerts." His daughter sang in the school choir, but Travis had never been around to attend any of the group's performances.

"Promise?" Charlie's mouth lifted in a half-smile.

"Cross my heart." He traced an imaginary X over his chest.

"Okay, I guess we can stay."

He grabbed Charlie's backpack with her sack lunch inside and they entered the building. The smell of disinfectant and lemon-scented cleaner greeted them as he ushered his daughter into the main office.

"May I help you?" A gray-haired woman in her fifties removed her bifocals. The nameplate on the desk read Rosie Finch.

"I'd like to register my daughter for school," Travis said.

"How nice. I hadn't heard we had a newcomer to town." Rosie opened a drawer and withdrew a packet of papers. "You'll need to fill out these forms." She smiled at Charlie. "What grade are you in, dear?"

"Second."

Rosie found a pen and filled in several blanks. "What's your name?"

"Charlotte Cartwright," Travis supplied.

Rosie's pen slid across the paper, leaving a trail of blue ink. "You're Dominick's son?" Evidently the news of Travis's arrival at the Lazy River had spread through the small town.

"That's correct. I'm Travis Cartwright."

Charlie stood on her tiptoes and peered over the counter at the woman. "I have the same name as my grandma, but everyone calls me Charlie."

Rosie's cheeks lost their pink hue as she stared at Travis. "I heard about your mother's passing. I'm so sorry."

"Thank you."

"I went to school with Charlotte." Rosie left her desk and stood at the counter. "Her father owned the bank in town. It was such a tragedy when Charlotte's parents drowned in a boating accident right before she married Dominick."

Travis wasn't in the mood to discuss his family history with a practical stranger. He checked his watch. "I'm in a hurry if we could—"

"Oh, certainly. Principal Edwards will wish to speak with you before Charlie's assigned to her classroom." Rosie entered the principal's office, closing the door behind her.

"Does everybody here know Grandma?" Charlie asked.

"Looks that way." Travis skimmed the forms, then began filling in the information.

"Dad." Charlie pointed across the room to the plate-glass window. "Here comes that schoolteacher lady."

Sara Sanders's shoulder-length hair curled softly around her face. She wore an ankle-length jean skirt with a camel-haired sweater that ended below her hips. A brown leather belt hung loosely around her waist, matching the color of her leather boots. There was no disguising her height or sturdy build, but dressed as a teacher she appeared feminine and touchable—not prickly as she had when she'd stopped in at the ranch to speak to Dominick before Thanksgiving.

It was only when she opened the office door and stepped inside that their eyes met. He swore he heard her breath catch. Obviously his presence had caught her by surprise. He nodded. "Ms. Sanders."

Sara shifted her attention to his daughter. "Hi, Charlie."

"Hi."

"I thought you were leaving town." Sara directed the question to Travis.

"Change of plans."

Charlie inched closer to the teacher. "We're gonna move into my grandpa's house and I'm gonna go to school here."

When Sara showed no reaction to the news, Travis added a few more details. "Dominick offered me a job troubleshooting his company's oil wells. As soon as Charlie's registered, I'm returning to Houston to pack up our house. I'll be back by Friday." When Travis accepted the job, he'd decided to rent his house in Houston and allow Charlie to finish the school year in Tulapoint. Hopefully by then he'd know whether he wanted to continue working for Cartwright Oil. If he did, then he'd sell the house and find a permanent home for him and Charlie around Tulapoint.

"Charlie," Rosie interrupted the conversation. "Principal Edwards would like to speak with you." The older woman whispered to Sara, "He's as handsome as Dominick was in his younger years." Grinning, Rosie led Charlie into the principal's office and shut the door.

Left alone with Sara, Travis asked, "How was your Thanksgiving?"

Her eyes twinkled, but she kept a straight face. "Probably not as interesting as yours."

He grinned. "Probably not." An awkward silence ensued, which caught Travis by surprise. Usually he had no trouble carrying a conversation with a woman. *Sara's not just any woman—she's the thorn in Dominick's backside.*

The principal's door opened and a short, stout man approached with his hand extended. "Thomas Edwards, principal of Tulapoint Elementary. Welcome to town." He motioned to Sara. "Ms. Sanders, you have a new student."

"Wonderful." Sara smiled at Charlie.

Things couldn't have worked out better if Travis had planned them. With Charlie being one of Ms. Sanders's students, Travis had a legitimate excuse to contact the teacher and become better acquainted with her.

"Rosie will need Charlie's files from her previous school and her immunization records," Edwards said.

"I had the school fax over the health forms this morning." Travis withdrew the papers from his coat pocket and handed them to Rosie. "They'll send the rest of her records in the mail."

"Ready to meet your new classmates?" Sara asked Charlie.

"I guess." Charlie edged closer to Travis.

"Remember, you're taking the bus home today and Juanita will pick you up at the end of the driveway." Travis dropped to one knee and pulled his daughter close. Charlie didn't protest. "Call me as soon as you get home from school," he said.

His daughter had her own cell phone—a present from him after her grandmother's death. He'd also bought Charlie three new Barbie dolls and probably would have kept giving her toys if she hadn't accused him of trying to make her stop crying.

"Ms. Sanders," Rosie said. "When I mentioned the class Christmas party, Charlie asked if her father could help out."

Way to go, Charlie.

"You said you wanted to do more stuff with me," Charlie reminded Travis.

"That I did." Travis could kill two birds with one stone—take an interest in his daughter's activities and find out why Sara Sanders and her brothers refused to do business with Cartwright Oil. "I'd be happy to help with the party."

"The room mothers and I are meeting Friday, after school, if you care to join us." The invitation lacked enthusiasm.

Travis hugged Charlie one more time. "Be good." He waved as his daughter left the office holding Sara's hand.

"I'm sorry about your mother's passing." The principal's apology sounded heartfelt. "I was three years behind Charlotte in school."

Rather than open the door for more questions, Travis said, "I should finish filling out these forms before I leave."

"If you have any concerns, don't hesitate to call or set up a meeting with me." Edwards slapped Travis on the shoulder, then retreated to his office.

"Would you care for a cup of coffee?" Rosie asked.

"No, thanks."

Left alone with his thoughts, Travis's mind wandered to Sara. The schoolteacher didn't like him, but that didn't mean she was immune to him. He'd felt her heated stare when she'd thought he hadn't been paying attention. He appreciated a certain amount of stubbornness in a woman and he admired Sara for standing her ground with a man like Dominick, but no matter that he found her intriguing, their relationship had to remain businesslike. He had too much on his plate to pursue the schoolteacher on a personal level. He had all he could handle learning a new job, trying to get to know his siblings, being a better father to Charlie and earning Dominick's respect by delivering Sara's agreement to sell the Bar T.

Time would tell how long Sara could resist his rough-neck charm.

SARA CHECKED THE CLASSROOM clock. 4:00 p.m. School had ended an hour ago. Evidently Travis Cartwright wouldn't be keeping his promise to attend the after-school meeting to plan the Christmas party.

"Sara?"

Startled, she tore her gaze from the clock. "I'm sorry?" She smiled at Darla Kemper, one of the room mothers seated at the children's worktable.

"I designed the invitations for the party next Friday." Darla displayed the elaborate artwork.

"They're beautiful." Sara wished Darla put as much effort into encouraging her son to do his homework as she did designing party invitations.

"We should put a reminder inside the invitations for the school food-bank project." Patsy Reynolds shared the room-mother duties with Darla. Sara appreciated the woman's common-sense approach to helping in the classroom.

"Good idea," Sara said. "Let's send the invitations home with the children on Monday." A few years ago, she'd done away with the traditional holiday gift exchange in her classroom and had the children bring in canned food for needy families in the community. The idea had been a huge success and now each grade participated in the food drive. This season, donations were down and the number of needy families had risen from twelve to eighteen.

"What about snacks for the party?" Darla said.

"How about a Victorian supper?" The mothers stared at Sara with blank faces. "Since we're reading Dickens' *A Christmas Carol*, I thought a Victorian-themed party would be nice."

Patsy shrugged. "Why not? I'll look up Victorian foods and prepare a sign-up list for the parents."

Bless you, Patsy.

"Oh, shoot. I need to go." Darla shoved her notebook into her purse. "Bob's pulling a double shift today. I'd better get home before the kids tear the house apart." Darla's husband owned a tow-truck business.

"What about the decorations?" Patsy asked.

"I've set aside time for the kids to make ornaments for the class tree." Sara walked the ladies to the door.

"Who's bringing in the Christmas tree?" Darla asked.

"I thought I'd see if the other room parent…" Sara sucked in a quiet breath when she glanced down the hallway and spotted Travis. "Here he is now."

"Wow. Wish I hadn't put on those extra ten pounds over Thanksgiving." Patsy sighed. "Not that it matters. A guy like that wouldn't give girls like us a second look, would he, Sara?"

Although Sara was used to people viewing her as a simple unadorned woman, Patsy's comment still stung.

"Hello, ladies," Travis greeted. "Sorry I'm late."

"You're helping with the Christmas party?" Darla asked.

"Yes, ma'am."

The deep timbre of his voice sent a shiver down Sara's spine—or maybe it was the heady scent of his cologne. She swallowed a sigh. The roughneck could *ma'am* her any day and all day. "Travis Cartwright, meet Patsy Reynolds and Darla Kemper." She motioned to each woman. "My room mothers."

"Nice to meet you, Travis. Gotta run." Darla rushed off.

Patsy scribbled her telephone number on a piece of paper and handed it to Travis. "Call me if you need help finding a tree." Patsy winked, then followed Darla.

Travis frowned at the note.

"Patsy's divorced with four children." Sara left out the obvious—the single mother was on the hunt for a husband. Sara wandered over to her desk and organized papers, willing her heart to cease pounding. Her memory of Travis hadn't done him justice. His broad frame filled out his cable-knit sweater, reminding her of a muscular New England fisherman.

He strolled around the classroom. "So this is Charlie's new home away from home."

"Her desk is over there." Sara nodded to the opposite side of the room.

"How did Charlie do this week? When I spoke to her on the phone, she sounded excited about school."

"She did great." Charlie had a rough first day when two boys had made fun of her name. After Sara had explained that Charlie's grandmother had recently died, the boys had decided that Charlie was a cool nickname for a girl. "She's made a new friend—Mary Parker. They eat lunch together and play during recess."

"Charlie mentioned Mary." Travis stopped in front of her desk. "Are you busy?"

"No." She'd planned to grade papers until five. "Why?"

"Would you like to grab a bite to eat?" His lips curled in a sexy half-grin. "You can tell me about the tree I've been assigned to find for the classroom."

For half a second Sara stopped breathing, then she chided herself for her silly reaction. Travis wasn't asking her out on a date. A man like him would never be interested in a woman such as herself. Good thing, because she had no intention of falling for another handsome man—been there. Done that. Paid a high price. When she was ready to dive into another relationship, she'd pick a steady Eddy, not a tall, muscular, tanned, handsome, sexy roughneck. "Patsy or Darla could give you a call next week," she said.

His expression sobered. "There's something else we need to discuss."

"Oh?"

"Dominick."

The mention of her pesky neighbor startled Sara like a cold splash of water in her face. She should have expected that Dominick would send his son to do his dirty work. Maybe dinner wasn't such a bad idea. By the end of the meal Travis would understand no one bullied Sara Sanders. "How about Beulah's?" she suggested.

"I'll wait for you in the parking lot."

As soon as Travis left the room, Sara's jittery nerves calmed. Even though she stood five-ten and weighed—never mind—Travis was still an imposing man. She gathered the student grammar tests and crammed them into her schoolbag, then put on her coat and flipped off the lights before shutting the classroom door.

When she reached the parking lot, she noticed Travis's truck idling in the spot next to her white compact. He flashed another smile—Lord, the man's teeth were white. She left the school, the truck's headlights burning into the back of her head. Ten minutes later she arrived at Beulah's and parked by the patio.

Beulah met them in the hallway when they entered through the back door. "Howdy, Sara."

"Beulah, you remember Travis Cartwright."

"Sure do. Where's that youngin' of yours?"

"With her grandfather," Travis said.

They were escorted into the front room and seated by the window. "You plan to stick around for a while?" Beulah asked Travis.

"Appears that way." Travis nodded across the table. "Sara is Charlie's new teacher."

"Ain't that interesting." Beulah snagged the pencil protruding from her beehive hairdo. "Ready to order?"

"I'll have the shepherd's pie and coffee."

"Make mine the same," Travis said.

"Be back in a jiffy."

As soon as Beulah walked out of earshot, Sara steered the conversation toward Christmas trees. "Last year, the room mothers purchased a real evergreen for the class party, but the tree dried out too quickly and became a fire hazard."

"What about an artificial tree?" Travis suggested.

"I was hoping for something more unique. Would you be able to come up with an idea for a homemade tree? Not too large—just big enough to hold thirteen ornaments?"

"Sure. Charlie and I will brainstorm something. When do you need the tree?"

"Next Friday."

Beulah delivered their coffee. "Food will be right up."

Christmas-tree talk exhausted, Sara avoided eye contact and sipped her coffee.

"How—"

"What's—" They spoke at the same time.

"You go first," he said.

"What's it like having a job in the middle of the ocean?"

"Not as glamorous as people assume. I worked the second shift—6:00 p.m. to 6:00 a.m. After I clocked out in the morning, I'd eat breakfast, then sleep until two."

"What did you do for entertainment?"

"Watched movies, played pool, Ping-Pong or lifted weights."

Her eyes strayed to his biceps—he must have lifted a lot of iron. "You didn't feel claustrophobic living in such close quarters?"

"Sometimes." He didn't elaborate.

"I imagine your coworkers will miss you." She wondered if any girlfriends would miss him, but Beulah returned with their food and a basket of warm bread, ending her line of questioning.

"You've lived here all your life, so you must know Matt and Samantha pretty well." Travis buttered a roll.

"My brothers and I helped around the ranch a lot and didn't have much of a social life outside of school." Mostly true. She saw no reason to share with Travis that his sister had been popular and had hung out with the in-crowd, while she'd been a bookworm with few friends. "How was your first Thanksgiving at the Lazy River?"

"Charlie had fun with her cousins."

Sara noticed Travis hadn't said whether he'd enjoyed the gathering.

"The recent Cartwright weddings have been the talk of the town," Sara said. "Duke this past February, then Matt in July and Samantha in September." Sara had been green with envy when she'd heard Samantha and Wade Dawson were tying the knot. Sara's wish to marry and have a family of her own seemed farther out of reach than ever these days.

"There's still one Cartwright sibling that's single." Travis winked.

Sara resisted the urge to ask why Charlie's mother wasn't in the picture, but the less she knew about Travis's personal life the better.

"How long has my father been after you to sell the Bar T to him?"

Travis didn't beat around the bush. "He hasn't told you the whole story?"

"Our schedules haven't allowed us to talk much."

"My father took out a second mortgage on the Bar T a couple of years ago. Around the same time his health took a turn for the worse. The medical bills piled up until he died this past April."

"I'm sorry."

"For what?"

"I didn't know that your father had passed away so recently."

His simple confession sounded more sincere than the five-hundred-dollar flower arrangement Cartwright Oil sent to the funeral home.

"Thank you. Before my father died, we'd commissioned a soil study on the property and the ranch tested positive for oil. We'd hoped to lease the drilling rights and use that money to get out of debt."

"What's kept you from going ahead with your plans?"

"Your father." At Travis's surprised expression, Sara explained. "I don't have proof, but I believe your father is wielding his influence and forcing the local oil companies to lowball their bids."

"That's not ethical."

"I keep forgetting that you never knew your father existed until recently. In time, you'll begin to see Dominick for what he really is."

Travis stiffened. "And what is that?"

"A bully." Sara breathed in deeply, hoping to calm her anger. "He's forcing our backs to the wall with the bogus lawsuit he recently filed. What your father refuses to understand is that no matter what he does, we're not selling or leasing to him."

"What's your backup plan?"

There was no backup plan. "Win the lottery." She waved a hand in front of her face. "I promised my father that Dominick would never step foot on the Bar T."

Pointing his fork at her food, he said, "Eat before it gets cold."

She was grateful Travis dropped the subject of oil, and they ate in silence.

"Apple pie?" Beulah topped off their coffee cups.

"No, thank you." She loved apple pie, but the extra calories would go straight to her hips.

"Bring two." As soon as Beulah walked off, Travis said, "You're not one of those women who never eats dessert, are you?"

She snorted. "Do I look like a woman who never touches sweets?"

His eyes twinkled. "I like a woman who appreciates good food."

No problem there. Sara craved all kinds of food—more than she should.

They ate dessert in silence and Travis grabbed the check as soon as Beulah set it on the table. "I'll pay for my meal," Sara said, digging through her wallet.

"It's on me." Travis tossed thirty dollars on the table.

"This isn't a date," she insisted.

He leveled his lethal grin at her. "Can't a friend pick up the tab this once?"

Friend? Travis Cartwright was dangerous to her health and heart. She had no intention of becoming friends with him.

Chapter Five

"Ms. Sanders says if I get all my spelling words right next time, she'll put my picture on the shining-star wall." Charlie dragged a chair to the kitchen counter, where Juanita measured ingredients for cookie dough.

This was the first Travis had heard of any *wall*. "What's a shining-star wall?"

"Kids who do something good get their picture on the bulletin board." Charlie rolled her eyes. "Bethany always gets her picture on the wall."

Ah, so his daughter was jealous of Bethany. "I'll quiz you on your spelling words after supper."

"That's okay. Grandpa said he'd help me when he gets home."

Travis ignored the sharp sting of Charlie's words. They'd lived at the Lazy River for two weeks and already his daughter believed Dominick walked on water. Travis and his father, on the other hand, were still feeling their way around one another—as if one wrong look or word would sever the invisible truce between them.

When Dominick had departed on his recent business trip, Travis had breathed a sigh of relief. He'd spent Monday and Tuesday at Cartwright Oil's corporate office in Tulsa, familiarizing himself with the various company oil rigs and their operational logs. No one had voiced an objection to Travis working for the company, except one field supervisor who made little effort to disguise his displeasure at being forced to relinquish some of his duties to Travis.

"Ms. Sanders says I'm as good a reader as Bethany and she's the best in the class." Charlie snuck a pinch of cookie dough when Juanita retrieved two eggs from the fridge.

"Ms. Sanders is a smart teacher," Juanita said, cracking an egg against the side of the sink.

Ms. Sanders this. Ms. Sanders that—the very woman responsible for Travis's grumpy mood. At the end of their impromptu dinner date at Beulah's this past Friday, he'd invited Sara out for coffee the following morning. His intention had been to show how harmless he was. He was confident that once he'd gained her trust, he could persuade her to do business with Dominick. Sara had turned down his invitation.

Not easily discouraged, he'd phoned the school on Monday and had left a message on the teacher's voice mail, inviting her to join him and Charlie for pizza that evening. She'd never returned his call. He'd phoned Sara Tuesday and had received the same response—none.

Travis wasn't a vain man, but most of the women he asked out jumped at the chance to be with him. That the schoolteacher had given him the cold shoulder both amused and frustrated him. Travis had to be careful how hard and heavy he pursued Sara—he didn't want to give her the idea he was romantically interested in her. Sara wasn't his type and he doubted she was into flings.

"Ms. Sanders said just 'cause I'm not big like the other kids it doesn't mean I'm not smart." Charlie wrinkled her nose.

"She's right. Size has nothing to do with brains," Travis said.

"Tell that to stupid Trevor. He thinks I have a tiny brain."

"Want me to beat Trevor up?"

Charlie's giggle warmed Travis's heart. He couldn't recall the last time he'd made his daughter laugh.

"Ms. Sanders made Trevor stay after school and wash all the desks."

Good for Ms. Sanders.

"And Ms. Sanders said she didn't get tall 'til high school." Charlie took the spoon Juanita handed her and scraped the remaining cookie dough off the sides of the mixing bowl. "Do you think I'm gonna be as tall as Ms. Sanders?"

Obviously Charlie was infatuated with her new teacher. "I don't think so, Charlie. Julie was only five feet three inches." Sara would tower over Charlie's birth mother, but if she stood toe-to-toe with Travis she'd almost stare him in the eye. *Perfect for kissing.*

Whoa. Where had that thought come from? Friends didn't kiss—not in the way Travis had envisioned a moment ago.

"Think I'll go for a drive." Since Sara hadn't returned his calls he'd head over to the Bar T and pay a visit to her brothers—maybe they'd be easier to sway than their sister. "Want to come along, Charlie?" He grabbed his jacket from a hook by the back door.

"Nope. I'm gonna help Juanita put the lights on the Christmas tree after we bake cookies."

Speaking of Christmas trees… "Think about what kind of tree you want to make for the class party this Friday. When I get back, we'll talk about it."

The Bar T Ranch was due north of the Lazy River. Travis drove along a frontage road, keeping his eyes peeled for the entrance. He'd gone a mile when he noticed Sara scuffling with a cow behind a barbed-wire fence. He checked the rearview mirror, then pulled onto the shoulder and shifted into Park. *I'll be damned.*

Sara was a sight to see in her hip-hugging blue jeans as she flailed her arms in the face of the steer and stomped her boots. The stubborn animal chewed its cud and stared right through her.

There were no other cows in sight, save the one receiving a dressing down from the schoolteacher. He turned off the truck and sidled up to the fence for a front-row view of the show.

"Blasted animal," she muttered. "Stupid brothers." A second later… "Damn all males to hell and back." She kicked a petrified cow pattie sky-high.

Travis backpedaled a few steps.

"Are you going to stand there and watch or help me convince this beast to head back to the herd?" Slowly, as if she didn't trust the bovine not to charge, Sara peeked over her shoulder.

"Shouldn't you be grading papers or something?"

"Gabe took off the day after Thanksgiving." She blew out a frustrated breath. "I came over after school to help Cole."

"What's wrong with the cow?"

"He's a renegade. No matter where the herd grazes, he wanders off."

"Why can't he eat where he wants?"

"Cole's inoculating the herd and this guy needs to be vaccinated."

Sara's car sat parked on the dirt road running parallel to the pasture. "You could tie the steer to the bumper on the car and drag him back to the barn."

"I'm tempted to, but this guy is so bullheaded I'd end up breaking his legs before he budged an inch." She waved her hands but the cow only blinked.

"How come you won't return my calls?" Travis asked. "I thought we had a nice time at Beulah's." Silence. "I was hoping we could get to know one another better." After watching her amusing struggle with the cow, he decided Sara might turn out to be a fun friend.

"Becoming friends isn't a good idea."

Was she on to him already? "Why?"

She gaped as if he'd lost his mind. "Dating the father of one of my students isn't...isn't...acceptable."

Dating? Who said anything about dating? At least she hadn't guessed his real motive. "Is dating the single father of a student against school rules?"

"No, but that's beside the point." She perched her hands on her hips. "Charlie's liable to get hurt."

"How do you figure that?"

A red flush crept up Sara's neck. "She won't understand when things don't work out."

They'd gone from getting to know one another to dating to breaking up in the span of sixty seconds. Taking pity on her, he dropped the subject and motioned to the steer. "Tell me what to do."

"Never mind. I'm sure you have better ways to spend your time than wrestling a cow."

"Not really. I was on my way to the Bar T to introduce myself to your brothers."

She balled her hands into fists and Travis wondered if she intended to punch the cow or him. A moment later, the steer moved—in the wrong direction. "Hey, come back here!" Sara trotted after the cow.

Now what—stand here and do nothing? Or make a fool out of himself and run after the animal? *What the hell.* Travis hopped the fence, then zigzagged around a minefield of cow patties as he sprinted ahead of Sara. He shouted and waved his arms. The cow stopped. Snorted. Changed directions and took off toward a gaping hole in the barbed wire.

"Don't let him get to the road!" Sara hollered.

The steer picked up speed and damned if Travis's lungs didn't burn trying to keep up. Tired of running, he launched himself at the animal, flinging his arms around its neck. He locked his knees, but the cow kept trotting and Travis swore his boot heels would be worn down to nothing by the time the beast gave in.

All of a sudden the cow did a three-sixty and Travis went airborne. He hit a patch of rocky ground, then sat in a daze, his butt numb, his palms skinned. He didn't have time to get on his feet before Sara's scream reached his ears.

"Travis, watch out!"

The demented steer charged. Travis rolled sideways in the nick of time, saving himself from being trampled. He crawled to his knees but had to pitch himself forward when the steer headed for him again. This time Travis ended up sprawled on his stomach.

Okay, bad boy. I'm pissed. He hauled his aching body upright and glared at the animal. The steer lowered its head and walked toward Travis.

Yeah, that's right. Surrender, you stupid side of beef.

Feeling damn proud of himself, Travis turned away and shouted, "I got him to give up!" No sooner had the words left his mouth than he felt a hard shove from behind. Travis fell to the ground—*again*.

Sara screamed like a banshee and harassed the steer until it backed off. The schoolteacher sure had a set of lungs on her. Once the animal stood at a safe distance, she dropped to her knees and patted him from head to toe. "Any broken bones?"

"I'm fine." His face inches from Sara's chest, Travis was more than fine. How had the schoolteacher's voluptuous bosom escaped his notice?

"Did you hit your head?"

Travis didn't have a chance to answer because Sara's eyes widened, then she pinched her nose and stumbled back.

"Eew!"

"What?"

She scooted farther away. "You smell like...poo."

He sniffed, then cringed. His clothes were covered with cow-patty debris. "You don't have to talk to me like I'm one of your third-graders," he teased.

"What do you mean?"

"*Poo?* You're a big girl. Use a big-girl word."

"Fine. You smell like...like..."

"Say it." He grinned. "I dare you."

Sara's cheeks puffed up like a blow-fish. "You smell like *shit*."

"Say it again."

She rolled her eyes. "Shit. Shit. Shiiit!"

"Feels good, doesn't it?"

She giggled, then kept giggling until the sound turned into a belly-laugh that led to a snort, then a gasp of embarrassment, which brought her right back to giggling.

Fascinated by the change in Sara's usual cool demeanor, Travis leaned forward, grabbed her by the shoulders and kissed her. When she didn't pull away, he pressed his lips more firmly to hers, nuzzling her cold cheek with his nose.

A horn rent the air, shattering the intimate moment. He studied Sara's dazed expression. *Damn.* He was out of his mind kissing the schoolteacher. Okay, he found her attractive—so what? That didn't mean he wanted to become romantically involved with her. Hoping she wouldn't jump to conclusions, he apologized. "Sorry, I got carried away."

Sara winced as she rose to her feet. Crap. Had he hurt her feelings or had she hurt something else when she'd come to his rescue?

"That's Cole." She waved her hand.

Her brother parked his truck and headed in their direction. When Cole reached them, he sniffed, then made an ugly face. "What stinks?"

"Travis, this is my brother Cole."

"I'd shake your hand but as you can see, I'm covered in—" Travis crawled to his feet "—cow poo."

Cole nodded, then spoke to his sister. "I was worried when you didn't come back right away."

"Travis stopped to help, but the steer got the better of him."

"Not much of a rancher, I guess," Cole said.

"I'm what you'd call a roughneck cowboy. I prefer to chase oil, not cows."

"So I heard." Cole spoke to Sara. "It'll be dark soon. You might as well head home." He tipped his hat to

Travis, then walked back to his truck, where he grabbed a rope to lasso the steer.

"Talkative guy," Travis muttered.

"Thank you for trying to help." Sara made a move to follow Cole, but Travis snagged her arm.

"Have dinner with me tonight." Afraid she'd assume the kiss meant more to him than it had, he added, "I'd like to discuss how Charlie's doing in school."

"Call Rosie and she'll set up a conference during my planning period."

"I was hoping to talk to you today."

"I'm sorry, Travis. I've got a roast in the Crock-Pot at home."

He'd never heard that excuse before. "Let your brother eat the roast."

"The roast and the Crock-Pot are at *my* house not the ranch."

"You don't live at Bar T?"

"No, I bought a home in town across from the railroad tracks and the grain depot near the school."

"You mean, that block of old Victorians?"

"The one missing all its shutters is mine."

Sara Sanders owned the run-down gray-and-white Victorian. Why was she living in a money pit that would take at least three or four decades to renovate? "I like roast."

"Pushy man."

He chuckled. "I've been called worse."

"Didn't I mention that dating isn't a good idea?"

Damn, he'd guessed right. Sara believed he was interested in her. He was, but not for the reasons she assumed. "It's not a date—it's a parent-teacher conference."

"Six o'clock at my place." She walked off, then stopped. "Travis."

"What?"

"I'm serious about the dating part."

Me, too. "I understand."

"And, Travis?"

"What?"

"That kiss never happened."

"I know." At least he and Sara were on the same page about their relationship. If only he hadn't kissed her—now there was no denying he was attracted to her. Acknowledging his attraction to Sara would force Travis to keep his guard up and remain focused on his mission.

Easier said than done.

HE'S EARLY.

Sara moved the living-room curtain and watched Travis park his truck in front of her house. Today had been the most embarrassing, wonderful, worrisome, exciting day in recent memory—and it wasn't over yet.

Her first glimpse of Travis beneath the glow of the streetlight stole her breath. She replayed in her mind the kiss they'd shared in the pasture, and her heart skipped a beat. She'd been kissed a few times in her thirty years but never had a man's mouth triggered mini-earthquakes in all her X-rated places.

Her reaction—rather, overreaction—to a simple kiss served to remind her that she had no business lusting after Travis. It didn't matter if he'd grown up away from the powerful influence of his father. Travis was a Cartwright—the enemy. She'd been fooled once by a smooth-talking, handsome man—no way would she travel that road again. This time she intended to keep her wits about her and not fall victim to a man's flirty compliments.

Before Travis shut the truck door, he reached into the cab and removed...flowers? *Darn him*. This wasn't a date.

She hurried into the front hall and checked her appearance in the antique mirror she'd purchased at an estate sale. Most days she wore little makeup, but tonight she'd dusted a smoky gray shadow over her eyelids and had added a touch of mauve color to her lips. Worried Travis might believe she'd dolled herself up for him, she'd skipped the perfume and dressed down in a pair of jeans and a navy crew-neck sweater.

The bell bonged. She drew in a steadying breath, then opened the door. "Hello, Travis."

"Wow that's ugly."

For a split-second she thought he meant her, then she caught him staring at the cat. She'd thought she'd locked her roommate in the laundry room. "That's Walter." She scooped up the cat and stepped aside so Travis could enter her home. "He adopted me."

One morning she'd opened the front door and found the black cat with orange spots lying on her porch, beaten and exhausted. There were bald spots in his fur, one eye had been damaged and couldn't be saved, so the vet had sewn it shut. A chunk of flesh had been missing from his ear, and his tail had been broken.

Once she'd nursed Walter back to life, Sara had intended to release him into the wild, but the cat had refused to leave the house. The one time she'd set him outside, he'd clawed deep scratches in the front door. Since then, he'd remained an indoor cat.

Travis lifted a hand to pet Walter, but yanked it back when the cat hissed.

"Not too friendly, huh, Walt?"

Sara closed the door, then set the cat on the floor. Walter ran off. She motioned to the standing coat rack in the corner and Travis hung up his jacket. The earthy scent of aged leather and musky cologne drifted beneath her nose—much more appealing than the eau de poo he'd worn earlier.

"For you." He held out a bouquet of daisies.

Daisies. Not roses. Roses were for lovers—daisies for friends, which she and Travis could never be.

"Thank you." Sara led the way into the kitchen. Travis hovered in the doorway while she arranged the flowers in a vase she confiscated from beneath the sink.

"Smells great. Do you cook real meals all the time?"

"Depends on what you call a real meal?" Sara wasn't a svelte woman. She liked three squares a day and saw no sense in starving herself thin when there were no men around that she was interested in. She placed the vase in the middle of the kitchen table.

"I grill a mean steak on the barbie. Other than that I'm not much of a cook." He shrugged. "Since my mother died, Charlie and I have lived on microwavable meals and boxed dinners."

"I'm sorry about your mother, Travis."

"Thanks. She was a huge help in raising Charlie."

"I've got beer in the fridge." She kept her brothers' favorite brands on hand for when they dropped by, which wasn't often. "Or there's iced tea."

"Beer's good."

When Travis helped himself to a beer, Sara studied his backside, appreciating the way the denim jeans hugged his butt and thighs. The black T-shirt pulled taut across his broad shoulders, and his biceps flexed as he unscrewed the cap on the bottle.

"Thanks for…" His words trailed off when he caught her staring.

Embarrassed, she mumbled, "I need to bake the rolls…" Travis blocked her path to the oven. His gaze slid down her body and Sara swallowed a groan when her breasts tingled.

"Navy looks good on you." He stepped aside, but only a few inches and her shoulder brushed his chest.

She slid the pan of rolls into the oven, then set the timer. "You said you wanted to talk about Charlie." She took the long way around the kitchen table to the sink.

"Tell me about this Trevor kid in her class. Charlie claims the boy makes fun of the size of her brain." He grinned.

"Trevor is Darla's son. You met Darla at the Christmas-party meeting."

"Is he a bully?" Travis leaned against the fridge, the action casual as if he'd lounged in her kitchen every day.

"He's not a mean boy. My guess is that he has a crush on Charlie."

"The kid's teasing the wrong girl. Charlie thinks boys are dumb."

Life would be simpler if Sara hated all men. "Let's sit in the living room until the rolls are ready."

"Nice Christmas tree," Travis said. He wandered

closer and inspected an ornament—a present from one of her students.

Sara didn't know why she bothered with a tree when there was no one besides her to appreciate it. Her brothers hardly noticed her holiday decorations. Sara sat at one end of the couch. "Aside from Trevor teasing her, has Charlie said anything to suggest she's having a difficult time in school?"

"No, that's what worries me."

"I don't understand," she said.

Travis joined her on the couch, keeping one cushion between them—close enough for her to enjoy the scent of his cologne, yet far enough away to avoid an accidental touch.

"Charlie's too happy," Travis said. "If you could have seen her right after my mother died, you wouldn't believe she's the same girl."

"Is it possible she's in denial about her grandmother's death and refuses to grieve?"

"I don't think so." He set the beer bottle on the table. "You certainly can do no wrong."

"Pardon?"

"Ms. Sanders this…Ms. Sanders that. Charlie believes you walk on water. Do you?"

"My brothers will vouch for the fact that I don't." Sara had noticed in class that Charlie sought her approval several times a day. "It's not unusual for a child to cling to certain people after they lose someone special in their lives."

"My daughter's clinging to you?"

"She's my shadow."

"I'll speak to her—"

"Please don't. With time, she'll settle in and become

more independent. I imagine she acts the same way around Juanita."

"Yeah, she likes hanging out with the housekeeper." He snapped his fingers. "Now I remember what I was going to ask you. Is it possible for Charlie to sing in the school choir? That was one of her favorite activities before her grandmother became ill."

"I'll speak to the music teacher. I'm sure she'd allow Charlie to join the group next semester."

"Thanks."

"The town gossips are having a field day speculating about your sudden appearance after all these years."

He chuckled. "What are the stories floating around?"

"One says you're an impostor who's after the Cartwright fortune." The obvious physical resemblance between Travis and Dominick had put that rumor to death.

"Go on."

"Then there are those who claim your mother discovered Dominick was having an affair and that's why she left the family."

"If that's true, then she never got over my father, because there was never another man in my mother's life."

"Mrs. Abernathy suggests—"

"Who's Mrs. Abernathy?"

"She's married to the manager of the bank in town. She suggested your mother left Dominick for another man but hadn't realized she'd been pregnant with you at the time."

"When I find out the answer, I'll let you know. So

far my father's managed to dodge my questions about his relationship with my mother."

"I imagine he's trying to come to grips with Charlotte keeping you from the rest of the family all these years."

"Mind if I ask you a personal question?"

Payback for her nosiness. "Depends on the question."

"Why did you buy this house?"

"I wanted to live in town."

That wasn't a complete lie. She'd also purchased the home hoping to attract a husband.

What no one had figured out was that Sara had hoped the old Victorian would soften her image. It was difficult to camouflage her height or hide her big-boned physique—the kind of woman expected to live and work on a ranch. So she surrounded herself with feminine doilies, turrets and gingerbread trim. The problem was that every man in Tulapoint had known her since childhood.

"How long have you lived in town?" he asked.

"Five years." She'd hoped to be married and have started a family by now.

The oven timer dinged, reminding her that she'd better feed Travis and send him on his way. She suspected her neighbors were keeping track of the time her guest spent in her home, and she cringed when she thought of the rumors that would greet her at school tomorrow.

Chapter Six

"Ms. Sanders isn't gonna like your Christmas tree, Dad." Charlie held a piece of rebar in place while Travis secured it with wire. They'd been working in the barn for over an hour after his daughter had arrived home from school Thursday afternoon. Charlie had tired of helping him fifty-five minutes ago.

"This isn't my tree," he said. "It's the classroom's tree."

"It's not even a tree." Charlie pointed to Dominick's old dog sleeping on a pile of hay in an empty stall. "Fred thinks it's stupid. Don't you, Fred?" The dog's ears perked, then he yawned and curled into a tighter ball.

"Did you ask Ms. Sanders if you could make an oil-rig tree?"

No, he hadn't. "Hey, you didn't come up with any suggestions, so I had to think of something myself. Besides, Ms. Sanders told me to surprise the class." He'd considered phoning Sara to discuss his idea, but his emotions were still running high after eating supper at her home last night.

Travis had witnessed a softer side to the school-teacher, which had caught him off guard. Maybe it had been her one-eyed cat or the lonely tree in the living room that had created an aura of vulnerability around her. Sara was strong, stubborn, compassionate and caring—a woman he could easily fall for. Not until he'd returned to the Lazy River later that night had he realized he'd forgotten to discuss selling the Bar T to Dominick, which raised a white flag in Travis's head.

There had been a lot of changes in his and Charlie's lives—his mother's death, moving to the Lazy River, his job with Cartwright Oil. Charlie starting over in a new school. Now wasn't a good time to become involved with a woman—but Sara wasn't just any woman. She was *Sara*.

"Ms. Sanders doesn't like surprises," Charlie said.

He'd thought his design clever, considering the town of Tulapoint was smack in the middle of oil country. Travis jiggled the contraption, satisfied the rebar was secure. "Help me attach the evergreen sprigs."

"The kids are gonna laugh at me." Charlie scooped up an armful of branches.

"I'll make a deal with you," Travis said. "If Ms. Sanders doesn't like the tree, I'll buy an artificial one."

Tomorrow he'd stop by the school before the first bell. If Sara objected to the tree, he'd have plenty of time to purchase a replacement before the party in the afternoon. He eyed his handiwork. "The evergreen branches give it some color."

Charlie glowered. "It's still ugly."

His daughter's grumpiness was wearing on him. He tested the four main legs of the structure, making sure they fit snugly into the plywood base. Once he'd secured the braces and attached the duck's nest at the top of the rig, he'd fashioned a star out of barbed wire. He liked the star. Charlie didn't, because she appeared ready to cry.

"Ah, honey." He pulled his daughter close for a hug. "What's the matter?"

"I miss Grandma." She snuggled her blond head against his chest.

"Me, too." The words burned Travis's throat. He was a crappy father. Just because Charlie appeared to be adjusting to her new life at the Lazy River, didn't mean she'd forgotten her grandmother. His daughter needed him now more than ever and all he'd been concerned with lately was winning favor with his father.

"Grandpa's the only one who's gonna like your tree." Charlie sniffed.

Dominick was due back from a business trip today and Travis couldn't wait to tell him what had happened at the Wellington Rig site this past Sunday. He'd shown up unannounced to inspect the rig and had detected a sudden change in drilling mud weight and temperature, which indicated the mud had been cut by surface fluids. He'd taken immediate action to correct the situation, thereby averting a dangerous blowout and saving the company millions of dollars, not to mention a few lives.

"Grandpa says he's glad you like oil 'cause Uncle Matt, Aunt Sam and Uncle Duke don't."

Travis assumed Dominick was happy he and Charlie had moved to Oklahoma, but the old man continued to avoid discussing the past. As much as Travis wished to be a member of the family, he wouldn't fully embrace his father or siblings until he learned why his mother had walked away from her life at the Lazy River and raised him as an only child.

"Grandpa says you're still really sad that Grandma died."

Was that the reason Dominick refused to discuss Charlotte—he sensed Travis would never believe anything he said because of the close bond Travis had shared with his mother?

"Is Grandpa right?" Charlie asked.

"Yeah, I'm sad, honey."

"Grandpa's sad, too."

"Did he tell you that?"

"No, but he stares at Grandma's picture a lot."

"What picture?" Travis hadn't noticed any photographs of his mother around the house.

"The picture he keeps in his desk drawer."

A twinge of sympathy gripped Travis. His first instinct had been to take his mother's side and assume Dominick had been at fault for the breakup of his parents' marriage. What if his mother had been the one to betray their marriage vows?

"Grandpa asked if Grandma ever got sad."

His mother had been very depressed the last six months of her illness. "What did you tell him?"

"That Grandma stopped smiling 'cause her cancer hurt so much. And guess what?"

Travis brushed the hair off his daughter's forehead. "What?"

"Grandpa's eyes got all shiny, and he hugged me."

At one time, Dominick must have loved Travis's mother. What had torn them apart? The answers to those questions would have to wait. Right now, it was time to lighten the mood. "Remember how you made Grandma laugh with your silly faces?"

"Grandma liked this one best." His daughter pushed the tip of her nose up to resemble a pig's snout and oinked.

Grinning, Travis said, "Let's finish the tree." He reached for another evergreen sprig when Charlie squealed.

"Grandpa, you're home!" Dominick hovered in the barn doorway, clutching his briefcase and a shopping bag. Charlie flung her arms around his legs.

Dominick placed a protective hand on Charlie's blond head. A zap of jealousy caught Travis by surprise and he swallowed a curse. He was a grown man. He didn't need a hug from his father. Shoving his feelings aside, he worried that Dominick had overheard his and Charlie's conversation.

"That's an interesting oil rig you've got there." Holding Charlie's hand, Dominick moved farther into the barn.

"Ms. Sanders told Dad to bring a Christmas tree for my class party."

Shrugging Travis said, "Ms. Sanders never specified a traditional tree."

"I like it." Dominick's eyes twinkled and his mustache quivered. Travis ignored the pleasant feeling his father's approval had triggered in his gut.

"What's in there, Grandpa?" Charlie tugged on the shopping bag.

"For you, Charlotte." Dominick handed Charlie a stuffed teddy bear with a red plaid bow around its neck.

Charlie was so thrilled she hadn't noticed that

Dominick used her proper name. "Thanks, Grandpa." She hugged the bear.

Travis stared at the stuffed animal, thinking life sure was strange. If his mother hadn't left the Lazy River Ranch, then Dominick might have brought home a teddy bear for him. Purchased a new Chevy truck for his sixteenth birthday. Or sent him to college. Who knows what kind of man Travis would have ended up becoming had he been raised by both his parents.

"I'm gonna play with my new bear." Charlie poked her head inside the horse stall. "C'mon, Fred." The old hound got up slowly and followed.

"I'm guessing Charlotte allowed Fred inside the house while I was gone," Dominick said.

"He sleeps on the bed with her."

Arthritis made it impossible for the dog to jump, so when Dominick left on his business trip, Travis built a set of steps to place next to Charlie's bed. Juanita donated an old bathroom rug, which Travis had cut into pieces and glued to the wood to prevent Fred from slipping when he climbed the doggie stairs.

Dominick chuckled.

"What's so funny?"

"I'd like to see the expression on Ms. Sanders's face when you present her with the class Christmas tree."

Travis and his father shared a rare smile. "Next time, she'll know better than to ask a roughneck for help."

"When's the party?"

"Friday."

"Tomorrow?"

Invite him. Travis nodded. "Charlie would like you to come."

"I'll be there for her."

Travis would have liked to have had a father there for him when he was growing up. "How was your business trip?"

"I renewed the leases on three wells."

Travis waited for Dominick to mention the incident at the Wellington rig, instead his father asked, "Have you convinced Ms. Sanders and her brothers to sell out to me?"

"They're accusing you of wielding your influence over the other oil companies and forcing them to—"

"Lowball their leasing bids."

"Are you?"

Dominick nodded. "Yes, I am."

"Bullying Sara won't get you far," Travis said. "She's determined to honor her father's dying wishes."

"So she's informed me."

"Will you consider negotiating a drilling lease instead of outright ownership of the property?" Maybe Sara would compromise—allow Dominick access to their oil, but ownership of the ranch would remain in the Sanders family.

"Why bother? The bank will eventually seize the Bar T. At which time, I'll purchase the property at a substantial discount."

"What if Sara changes her mind and accepts one of your competitor's bids?"

"I'm listening," Dominick said.

"Make the Sanders an offer they can't refuse." When his father didn't respond, Travis said, "Before you go any further with the lawsuit, let me see if Sara would be willing to discuss drilling rights instead of ownership."

Travis stiffened. Would Dominick approve of his strategy or laugh it off?

"Fine. I'll wait on the lawsuit until you've had a chance to talk sense into that gal." Dominick shifted his briefcase to the other hand. "Anything else eventful happen in my absence?"

His kissing Sara in a cow pasture had been eventful, but Travis

doubted his father would appreciate that tidbit of news. "Nope."

"Modest one, aren't you? Must have inherited that trait from your mother."

Had Dominick just given his mother a backhanded compliment? "What are you talking about?"

"The Wellington rig."

Secretly pleased his father intended to acknowledge his work, Travis said, "I was glad I discovered the problem before—"

"I heard the rig foreman gave you a hard time."

Samuel Pickett had done more than challenge Travis's judgment—the man had taken a swing at him when Travis had accused the foreman of cutting corners and jeopardizing the safety of his crew. Two of the derrick hands had stepped in and prevented an all-out scuffle.

"Your actions saved me hundreds of thousands of dollars in repairs, not to mention employee lives."

"All in a day's work."

"You remind me of my father," Dominick said.

"How so?"

"You two have the same temperament. Your grandfather's first name was Wellington."

"Did my grandfather purchase the Lazy River Ranch?"

"No. Wellington Cartwright didn't believe in putting down roots. He moved me and your grandmother all over Oklahoma in order to keep watch over his wells."

"How did he die?"

"A blowout."

The blood drained from Travis's face. "What was he doing on the platform?"

"Your grandfather liked the feel of warm crude on his hands. He insisted that I attend college, because he wanted me to run the company while he worked in the field." Dominick eyed Travis. "I bet you love changing drill bits and adding lengths of pipe just like your grandfather did."

"Physical labor has never bothered me."

"I'd just graduated from college when he was killed. As soon as the funeral was over, your grandmother packed her things and moved to California to live with her sister. I visited from time-to-time and made sure she never wanted for anything. But we didn't discuss Cartwright Oil after my father died."

"Is my grandmother still alive?"

"She died a few months after Matt was born." Dominick picked at a piece of lint on his sport coat. "Would you like to go to college?"

College? Was Dominick hoping Travis would to take over the company one day?

"You're not too old if that's what you're thinking," Dominick said.

"I know." How did Travis explain that he wasn't sure he wanted such a huge responsibility—to secure and expand a fortune that would provide for future Cartwright generations.

"I see." Dominick's shouldered stiffened.

"See what?"

"You haven't decided whether or not you're sticking around."

His father was a mind reader.

"You'll let me know when you decide, won't you?"

His father turned away, but Travis called after him. "Did you have an affair on my mother? Is that why she left you?"

The sorrow in Dominick's eyes sucked the wind from Travis's lungs. He watched his father leave the barn, wondering why he felt as if he'd just kicked the legs out from under poor old Fred.

PARENTS, GRANDPARENTS and younger siblings "oohed" and "aahed" over the children's Victorian-era drawings displayed on the walls of Sara's classroom. The play had gone off without a hitch and now everyone was socializing until the final bell rang.

"The plum pudding is a huge hit." Darla nodded at the kids sporting chocolate rings around their mouths.

The room mothers had put their own twist on the Victorian meal. Instead of roasted goose, there was ham and turkey lunch meat. And rather than provide the traditional drink, wassail, they decided on juice boxes.

"I can't believe he made an oil derrick instead of a Christmas tree," Patsy grumbled, joining Sara and Darla behind the teacher's desk.

Sara studied the green-colored rebar monstrosity and reined in the urge to laugh. Victorian ornaments hung from the crossbars of the structure and Santa's toy sack rested in the bird's nest at the top. "Mr. Cartwright meant well." Her eyes searched the room for Travis. He knelt next to Charlie's desk while she showed him her Victorian picture book.

Patsy and Darla rambled on about the oil derrick, but their voices faded as Sara's thoughts centered on Travis. Most of the parents had dressed up for the party, but Travis appeared every inch the roughneck in a flannel shirt, faded jeans and scuffed work boots—unlike his father. Dominick wore a Western suit with a bolo tie and polished cowboy boots.

A feeling of being watched sent a tingle down Sara's spine. No wonder—Dominick stared at her from across the room. *Darn.* Had the old coot caught her ogling his son? Dominick lifted his punch cup in salute and Sara dipped her head, acknowledging the silent message in his eyes—*I want your ranch.*

Shifting her attention to the room mothers, Sara pretended to listen. Why did Travis have to be so attractive and make her feel feminine and desirable? Another man's face flashed before Sara's eyes and her insides twisted at the memory.

Josh had been Travis's twin—handsome, nice, caring. He'd doted on Sara and she'd fallen for every lying word he'd uttered. Josh had promised her marriage, children and a happy-ever-after. She'd learned the hard way that men like Josh didn't fall for women like her. Josh had used her. He'd betrayed her trust, then had left her brokenhearted.

Travis is different.

Sara's heart yearned to believe Travis genuinely liked her, regardless of the fact that he could find a much slimmer, sexier, prettier woman. She wanted to believe he enjoyed her company and found her amusing and fun to be with—because darn it, she liked being with him.

Shoving thoughts of Travis aside, Sara forced herself to mingle and thank the parents—one in particular—for the bags of groceries that lined the classroom wall. As soon as the school day ended, she'd load up her car and deliver the food to Beulah's. Each year, Beulah helped organize the food donations for needy families. More often than not, she added items from her restaurant pantry to complete the holiday meals.

"I enjoyed the class play, Ms. Sanders." Dominick's voice startled Sara. The curmudgeon had snuck up on her.

"The children worked very hard to memorize their lines."

"It's been years since I've stepped foot inside this school and now I have two grandchildren attending."

"Did you have an opportunity to visit Luke's classroom?" Samantha and Wade's son was in Sheila Barns's fourth-grade class down the hall.

"I stopped in before heading here. Mrs. Barns appears to have a handle on Luke's academics."

The boy's high I.Q. might have been a problem in the classroom if not for Sheila creating an extra set of weekly plans specifically designed to challenge Luke.

When Dominick appeared in no rush to mosey along, Sara asked, "Did you enjoy Luke's class play?"

He nodded. "The Grinch is my favorite."

No doubt.

"The food drive was a success." Dominick pointed at the grocery bags.

Go on, say it. "Thank you for the generous donation

this year." Charlie had come to school with a check for one thousand dollars. Sara had been amazed Dominick had allowed his granddaughter to carry the bank draft in her lunch box. Because of his money, the needy families would receive enough food to feed them from now through Christmas.

"Glad I could help." Dominick nodded at Charlie. "I'd better visit with my granddaughter, then check back in on Luke."

As soon as Dominick walked off, Travis approached her—no escaping the Cartwright men. He studied her outfit, his eyes darkening with appreciation. "Nice costume."

Suddenly Sara was glad she'd rented the Victorian dress from a costume shop in Tulsa. The green velvet material weighed at least ten pounds and the tight-fitting bodice made drawing a deep breath difficult, but she'd wear the outfit everyday if Travis eyed her like a piece of candy.

"I spoke with Dominick about his lawsuit against you and your brothers."

"Is he going to drop it?" she asked.

"He agreed to hold off on it and give you more time to think about selling."

"We've been over this before, Travis. I'm not—"

"Dominick's open to negotiating drilling rights instead of ownership of the Bar T."

Sara refused to discuss Dominick or oil in her classroom. "I'm delivering the groceries to Beulah's after school. You're welcome to tag along and we can talk then."

"Fine. I'll send Charlie home with her grandfather."

Thirty minutes later, the school bell rang and the classroom emptied, leaving Travis standing by the door with a gleam in his eyes that both excited and worried Sara.

Chapter Seven

She's stalling.

Travis studied Sara as she wiped down the classroom desks for the second time in less than fifteen minutes. He made her nervous—probably because he couldn't stop staring at her.

The students and their parents had departed the Christmas party a half hour ago. While he'd loaded the grocery bags into his truck bed, most of the teachers had left the building. "Finished?"

"The carpet needs to be vacuumed."

Wasn't that the custodian's job? Travis counted to five, then exhaled slowly. "Beulah might be wondering where you are."

"I should change first." She smoothed her hands over her green velvet dress.

"No, you shouldn't." The tight-fitting bodice emphasized Sara's generous bosom and the cinched waist made her appear delicate and feminine. "Leave the dress on."

Offering a hesitant smile, Sara grabbed her coat and purse and joined Travis in the doorway. He pointed to the mistletoe above their heads, wondering if he could tease Sara into cooperating. "I've never kissed a woman beneath the mistletoe."

Sara peeked at the dangling sprig, her cheeks turning pink. What the heck. He tilted his head and moved in slowly, allowing her plenty of time to turn her head. She didn't. He brushed his mouth across hers in a whisper of a kiss. He pulled back and swore he read disappointment in her eyes.

They strolled down the corridor in silence. When they reached the parking lot, he opened the driver-side door of his truck and helped Sara inside. Her cool fingers slid across his palm and a jolt of electricity shot up his arm. There was no denying he was physically attracted to the schoolteacher. As long as his interest in Sara remained solely physical, he didn't see a problem in trying to influence her to do business with Dominick.

Once he started the engine, he adjusted the temperature inside the cab. "The Christmas party was a success."

"You've mentioned that three times now."

He had? "Which families will benefit from all this food—or is that a secret?"

"Tulapoint outlawed secrets decades ago. I'm sure the news of you helping to deliver the groceries to Beulah's has already been broadcast across county lines." She waved a hand in the air. "Thanks to your sister, the town no longer has to help one of its residents."

"Who's that?"

"Millicent, the local water witch. She lives on Samantha and Wade's new ranch."

"People still believe in water witches?" Travis backed out of the parking spot and left the school.

"Wade wasn't a believer until Millicent's willow

switch located water for a new well." Sara shifted toward Travis. "Have you and Charlie visited Last Chance Ranch? Samantha and Wade did an incredible job renovating the old Peterson farmstead."

"I promised Charlie we'd drop by Samantha's ranch and see the rescued horses this weekend." Travis had put off visiting his sister, using work as an excuse. He was still uncomfortable around his siblings. They had little in common—Samantha and Matt had been raised in the lap of luxury and Travis had had to earn his own way. He had to get over that if he intended to make a new life for him and Charlie in Tulapoint.

At the edge of town, he turned onto the rural road that led to Beulah's. "So this water witch has lived on the property forever?"

"It's believed Millicent is close to a hundred years old. Her parents were sharecroppers on the Peterson farm. She married a man in the military service but her husband died shortly after being shipped overseas, leaving her a pregnant widow. She stayed with the Petersons as their housekeeper and cook until the older couple died."

"What happened to her son?" Travis asked.

"He left home in his late teens and never returned. He might have passed away by now. Millicent doesn't talk about him."

Travis felt sorry for the old woman. "No family. That's rough."

"Samantha, Wade and Luke are her family now."

"Mind if I change the subject?"

Her eyes narrowed. "Go ahead and give me your best sales pitch from your father."

"Dominick's willing to buy drilling rights and leave the property to you and your brothers."

"I doubt your father will be content with leasing a few wells from us. He won't be happy until he owns the entire state of Oklahoma."

"You're running out of options."

Sara's sigh echoed through the cab. "I'll speak to my brothers about negotiating a lease, but not until Dominick makes an official offer."

"Fair enough." Travis backed off, feeling confident he'd made substantial progress in helping Sara and his father negotiate a business deal.

A quarter mile passed before Sara spoke. "How do you like working for your father?"

"So far so good." Actually, things were going better than Travis had anticipated. His father was keeping his distance and allowing Travis some breathing room.

"Do you miss your old job?" Sara asked.

"I miss the guys I worked with, but I like the freedom my new job has." Travis enjoyed traveling to different rigs, but there was little opportunity to get to know the crews real well. His salary went a long way in making up for the lack of camaraderie.

"What do you and Charlie have planned for her winter break from school?"

"Charlie keeps dropping hints that she'd like to visit one of her old friends in Houston."

"I imagine you have friends—" Sara put just the right amount of emphasis on the word *friend* to indicate she referred to female companions "—that miss you."

"My last serious girlfriend was Charlie's mother. After Julie took off I've stuck to—" *one-night stands* sounded crude "—casual dating. What about you?"

Weren't most women who lived in small towns married by Sara's age?

"I was engaged once."

She didn't elaborate, so he prodded. "Don't leave me hanging."

"It didn't work out."

"That's all you're going to say?"

"What more do you want to know?"

"Everything." He shouldn't care about Sara's personal life, but the more time he spent with her, the more intriguing he found her.

"Josh—which wasn't even his name. He used an alias. Worked as a ranch hand for my father. He was handsome and funny. I fell in love with him and he led me to believe that he returned my feelings. He proposed. I said yes and then one morning he was gone." She winced as if the memory physically hurt her.

Even though Travis had never met the guy, he wished he could punch the cowboy for hurting Sara. "He get cold feet?"

"No. He used me to learn his way around the ranch, then when our backs were turned, he took off with our prized breeding bull and we never saw him again."

Travis felt bad that Sara had been used that way. "I'm sorry. The guy's a schmuck." For a split-second he worried that he was leading Sara on, then he discarded the notion. He wasn't disappearing after Sara and his father negotiated a drilling lease and he had every intention of remaining friends with her.

Sara changed the subject. "So you never married Charlie's mother?"

"No. I proposed, but Julie avoided setting a wedding date. That should have been my first clue that she didn't

intend to stick around after she gave birth to Charlie."
He shrugged. "A week after we brought Charlie home
from the hospital, she split."

"She abandoned her baby?"

"Yep. No note. No forwarding address and she'd
canceled her number on our cell-phone plan, so there
was no way to get in touch with her." Travis had more
in common with his father than he'd first realized, each
of them having been involved with a woman who'd
abandoned their child or children as was the case with
Travis's mother.

"My daughter and I are better off without Julie." Had
Dominick felt the same way about Travis's mother?

"Are you worried Julie might return and try to seek
custody of Charlie?"

"If Julie wants to be part of Charlie's life at some
point in the future I won't protest, but there's no way
I'll allow Julie legal custody of our daughter." With the
Cartwright fame and fortune, Travis was confident his
ex-wife wouldn't stand a chance in a court of law if she
sought her parental rights.

"You and your mother have done a terrific job raising
Charlie. She's a sweet little girl."

"My mom gets most of the credit." He paused, then
changed the subject. "Do you picture yourself getting
married one day?"

"I hope so, but finding a man who wants to settle
in a small town isn't easy." She expelled a quiet sigh.
"Jobs are scarce around here unless you work in oil or
with cattle."

Beulah's pink Victorian came into view and Travis
turned into the driveway that led to the parking lot in
the back. "Speaking of things to do..." He shifted the

truck into Park and turned off the ignition. "How would you like to accompany Charlie and me when we visit Samantha's ranch tomorrow?"

"I don't want to interfere with your family time." Sara reached for the door handle, but Travis snagged her dress sleeve.

He leaned across the seat, his mouth hovering over hers, their breath mingling...steaming up the inside of the truck. "Spend the day with Charlie and me."

Maybe it was the fact that they'd both been burned by love. Or that she was too darn sexy in her Victorian dress. Or that he'd been left wanting more after their peck beneath the mistletoe. Whatever the reason, he ignored the voice in his head insisting he keep his personal feelings for Sara in check and pressed his lips to Sara's.

Soft...slow...deep. "Please."

Sara smiled. "You sure know how to beg."

"I'M JEALOUS." SAMANTHA joined Travis outside the round pen on her ranch.

For the past ten minutes he'd watched Sara attempt to coax Charlie onto the back of a horse called Snickers. "Jealous of what?"

"Not what. Whom." Samantha nodded at Sara. "I wanted to be the one to teach my niece how to ride, but it appears Charlie's become attached to her teacher." Samantha nudged Travis in the side. "What's going on between you two?"

"Between who?"

His sister rolled her eyes. "Sara Sanders. Dad's arch enemy."

Travis couldn't take his eyes off Sara. She wore

jeans, which showed off her ample curves and a sweater that left no doubt she was female. Sara was the kind of woman who wouldn't break in a man's arms and Travis found that sexy and distracting.

"Nothing's going on between us. We're friends." He cringed at the statement. His dream about Sara last night had been far beyond *friendly.*

"Sara's good with Charlie."

"Yes, she is." Travis believed the extra attention Sara showered on his daughter was one of the reasons Charlie was in better spirits these days. As a matter of fact, he worried that his daughter had acclimated too easily to life at the Lazy River. If his job with Cartwright Oil didn't pan out, he'd have a heck of a time uprooting Charlie and moving her back to Houston.

"Hey, Dad! I'm riding all by myself!"

"Hold on tight!" Travis grinned. Since he'd met his siblings, Travis's conversations with them had been more formal than familiar. Maybe it was time to move forward. "Has Dominick ever told you or Matt why our mother left him?" Travis was eager for any information that would help him understand his mother's actions.

"Matt and I have asked about Charlotte through the years, but Dad doesn't go into detail. He sticks with the same answer—'your mother wasn't happy, so she left.'" Samantha nodded toward the pen. "What does Dad think about you hanging around Sara?"

Obviously his sister didn't care to discuss their mother. Travis didn't want to upset her, so he went along with the change in subject. "It was Dominick's idea that I get closer to Sara. He wants me to convince her to negotiate a business deal with him."

Samantha sucked in a quiet breath. "You're leading her on?"

"No one's leading anyone on." Travis ignored the twinge that pricked his conscience. He had more than friends on his mind when he thought of the schoolteacher these days.

"Is Sara coming around to Dad's way of thinking?"

"She's considering negotiating a lease with Cartwright Oil if the price is right, but I haven't had a chance to speak with Dominick about how high he's willing to go."

"After you come to an agreement, what then? Do you plan to go public with your relationship?"

"Relationship? We're not even dating."

Samantha laughed. "You can't stop staring at her."

Travis didn't have an opportunity to respond before Sara led Snickers in their direction. "Isn't Charlie doing a terrific job?" she said.

"Yeah, I'm terrific, aren't I, Aunt Sam?"

"You sure are, honey. Hey, Uncle Wade and Luke are home."

All eyes shifted to the gravel driveway, where a cloud of dust rose in the air. "I wanna play with Luke," Charlie said. Sara helped Travis's daughter down from the horse. "Thanks for teaching me to ride, Ms. Sanders." Charlie squeezed between the pen rails and raced across the yard, waving to her cousin.

"If you two want to go for a horseback ride, Wade and I will watch the kids," Samantha said.

"Ever ridden a horse?" Sara asked Travis.

"No, but I hear you're a pretty good teacher."

"That's the worst pick-up line I've ever heard." Samantha walked off, shaking her head.

Travis caught the scent of Sara's perfume as she edged closer to the rails. "Are you up for a riding lesson?" she asked.

"I'm up for any lesson you have in your planner." One day he'd love to show Sara exactly how good a student he could be.

HORSES GRAZING NEARBY, Sara and Travis lounged in the sun near the bank of a small pond on his sister's property.

"This is nice." Sara stared at the cloudless blue sky.

Travis rolled to his side, wincing.

"Sore?"

"Yeah, the rump's a tad tender."

Travis had been a quick study when she'd demonstrated how to use the reins. He might be a roughneck but he rode like a real cowboy—slouched low in the saddle, lean hips swaying to the rhythm of the horse's gait. "You're a natural."

His lazy grin sent her heart stumbling.

Don't even think about it. Startled by the voice in her head, she dropped her gaze to her lap. Something about Travis—his smile, the soft glow in his eyes when he watched his daughter, that same glow intensifying when he stared at her—begged Sara to allow him to get closer to her. She'd trusted a man once before and had been fooled by his handsome face and purple prose. She'd rather be alone than risk heartache again.

Josh was four years ago. You're wiser. Stronger. A better judge of character.

Maybe she should consider an affair—no expectations. No messy emotions. Females all over the world engaged in sexual flings and one-night stands and survived the experience. The idea had merit, but Sara was too old-fashioned. She didn't want to give herself to a man unless she was certain he loved her and she loved him. After her experience with Josh, she'd lost confidence in her instincts where men were concerned.

Travis isn't Josh. She feared the more time she spent with Travis, the more she'd find to admire, respect and appreciate in him. Before long she'd find something to love about him and then she'd be in big trouble.

Needing to lighten the mood she nudged his shoulder. "Tell me more about life on an oil rig."

"Why so curious?" he asked.

"It's different from my job as a schoolteacher." All those strong, muscular, tanned men working in rough, dangerous conditions seemed…well, romantic.

"It's a lot more dangerous than people realize."

"How?"

"Not a week goes by that one of the crew members doesn't get hurt. Most injuries aren't serious, but some are. And there's always the risk of exposure to chemicals and gas leaks. Once in a while you hear about a helicopter going down in the ocean while ferrying oil workers back and forth between the rigs and the mainland."

Until Travis mentioned helicopters, Sara hadn't given much thought to how the crew members got to and from the oil platform.

"We work in difficult conditions. High winds and rain. Hands become stiff from the cold and it's easy to lose our grasp on the equipment. Once, I helped install a length of pipe and the support chain snapped."

"What happened?"

As soon as the question left her mouth, Travis removed his jacket and pulled his shirt tail from his jeans. He turned away and she gasped. "The chain whacked me across the back and knocked me to the deck. I was stunned and couldn't move out of the way in time to avoid the end of the pipe rolling over my leg. I was out six weeks with a broken ankle and two cracked ribs."

Sara caressed the puckered scar that dissected his back. "I'm amazed a blow like that didn't break your spine." Realizing how intimately she touched him, she yanked her hand back. His shirt fell into place and she curled her fingers against her palm, savoring the heat from his skin.

"A couple of years later—" he wiggled the pinky finger on his left hand and she noticed the digit was missing its tip "—this happened."

She mentally added courageous to Travis's list of admirable qualities. "You're very brave."

"My sister's the one with all the guts," he said.

"Samantha told you about her accident?"

"Yeah, and Dominick filled in the details. He said she'd been hosing down a horse when he spooked and kicked out, catching her in the head."

"No one thought she'd live. Her recovery amazed the doctors," Sara said.

"It's too bad Samantha still has trouble with her memory."

"The gossipmongers believe—" so did Sara, but she kept her opinion to herself "—that Wade's the reason Samantha's memory has improved dramatically these past few months." The love in Wade's eyes when he looked at his wife almost made Sara believe fairy-tale endings were possible.

"Real love heals all wounds, I guess." Sara studied Travis out of the corner of her eye. What if she and Travis fell in love—could that love heal decades of hurt and animosity between their families? *Dream on.* There was no happy-ever-after in the cards for the Cartwrights and the Sanders.

"Everybody's got their own definition of real love." Travis stared into the distance. "When I think of Julie walking out on Charlie after she was born and my mother abandoning two of her children and raising me alone…" He frowned. "How is that real love?"

"Some women aren't cut out to be mothers." The possibility of never marrying and having a child of her own bothered Sara deeply. She loved her students and enjoyed nurturing them in the classroom, but she wanted a son or daughter of her own to love. "You've shown Charlie real love."

"You're wrong." Travis grasped Sara's hand and squeezed. "I've failed Charlie. Before my mother died, I believed I was doing right by my daughter. I brought home a paycheck. Kept a roof over her head. Clothes on her back. Food on the table. But I left the parenting to my mother."

Then Charlotte died.

"I'm winging it with Charlie." Travis got to his feet and stood at the water's edge. "I came here with a grudge against my father only to learn he didn't even know I existed all these years. I don't have that excuse. I lived in the same house as Charlie and I still spent very little time with her."

"You're making up for that now." Sara joined him. "Don't be too hard on yourself. Now that your mother's gone, you and Charlie will form a different, better, closer relationship. Give it time."

"Hey, you guys!" Samantha called out as she approached on horseback. Once she dismounted, she said, "Thought I'd find you two here."

"Is something the matter with Charlie?" Travis asked.

"The kids are fine. Wade's playing Yahtzee with them." Samantha waved a fancy black envelope in the air.

"What's that?" Travis asked.

"An invitation to the annual Oilmen's Christmas Ball in Tulsa."

The ball was scheduled for the last Saturday before Christmas—next week. The party was considered *the* social event of the season in Tulsa.

"Dad expects you to be there." Samantha blushed. "I meant to tell you about it last week, but I forgot until Wade asked me a short while ago if you were coming."

Travis scuffed his boot against the ground. "I'm not a fan of big shindigs."

Sara's heart plunged at his words. A tiny part of her had hoped he'd agree to go to the ball, then ask her to accompany him. She'd never attended a high-society event and would love to experience a lavish evening of dancing and dining.

"I'll sit this one out, Sam," Travis said.

"You have to attend." Samantha slapped the envelope against his chest. "Dad plans to introduce you to all the movers and shakers in the oil industry."

Sara held her breath. *C'mon, Travis. Say you'll go. Then ask me to be your date.*

"You work for Cartwright Oil. The company executives will expect you to be there," Samantha insisted.

"I won't fit in."

"If you wear a tux, no one will believe you were a roughneck." Samantha glanced at Sara. "Right?"

Fighting a smile, Sara said, "Your sister makes a valid point. You're working for Cartwright Oil now."

"Fine. I'll go. But—" Travis turned to Sara "—you got me into this. The least you can do is be my date."

Heart pounding, Sara opened her mouth to accept, then chickened out. "I can't."

"Why not?" Travis and Samantha spoke in unison.

"Dominick will be upset if a Sanders crashes his party."

"Dad won't dare make a scene in front of all his business associates," Samantha said.

Sara made one last feeble protest. "There isn't enough time to find a dress before Saturday."

"I'll take you shopping in Tulsa," Travis said.

Dress shopping with Travis was out of the question. "I'll be your date for the ball." She raised a warning finger. "But I'll find my own dress." Sara prayed she'd stumble upon something suitable on a clearance rack for under a hundred dollars.

Chapter Eight

"Oh, dear." Tulapoint's lone hairstylist chewed her lip as she eyeballed Sara from head-to-toe.

"Oh, dear, what, Mazy?"

"We have a lot of work to do."

Sara yawned and rubbed her swollen eyes. "I didn't sleep well." She hadn't gotten a wink of rest last night—tossing and turning in bed, fearing she'd humiliate herself tonight at the Oilmen's Ball.

She'd spent the week following her visit to Samantha's ranch attempting to talk herself out of attending the social event with Travis. If not for her busy schedule at school, she might have had time to conjure up a good excuse. But before she knew it, winter break had arrived and here she was expecting Mazy to work miracles and transform her from a plain boring schoolteacher to a stunning debutante.

Mazy pushed open the screen door and motioned Sara inside. "Hurry, before someone sees you."

The enclosed back porch had been converted into a hair studio. Mazy and her fifteen-year-old son lived with her mother, who'd been a widow for as long as Sara had known Mazy. Their white clapboard house sat at the edge of town off the main road.

"Sit." Mazy motioned to the salon chair at the far end of the porch, then disappeared into the kitchen. A minute later, she reappeared with two pieces of fresh-cut cucumber, which she laid over Sara's eyes. "That should help the puffiness. Concealer will hide the dark circles."

"Thanks for agreeing to do my hair on short notice." Sara had booked the appointment an hour ago when she'd faced reality and accepted that she couldn't back out on Travis at the last minute.

"No problem. Mom took Billy to that fancy skateboard park in Tulsa. All I had on my agenda was housecleaning and I'd rather cut hair any day than scrub toilets."

Mazy's ex had left her for another woman two years after Billy had been born. "Is Billy spending Christmas with you or his dad?"

"Me. Neil's driving his wife and stepchildren to Arkansas so she can be with *her* family."

Hoping to avoid a drawn-out discussion of Neil's failings, Sara asked, "Did you finish your Christmas shopping?"

"Yes, but I need to pick up a few stocking stuffers." Mazy peeled off the cucumbers and shoved a hair-color chart into Sara's hands. "Blond or red?"

"Blond or red what?" Sara stared at the fake hair samples glued to the cardboard.

"Highlights. I'm thinking blond." Mazy fluffed the hair along Sara's jawline. "Blond will frame your face and emphasize your brown eyes."

Sara was reluctant to draw attention to any part of her body, but she desperately wanted to make an impression on Travis and if that meant going a little overboard, then she would. "Blond it is."

"Next question." Mazy set aside the hair-color samples. "Conservative or sexy?"

There was a fine line between sexy and trampy. What the heck. "Sexy."

While Mazy mixed the hair dye, she pummeled Sara with questions. "Describe your dress. Is it cut low in the back or the front?" When Sara didn't immediately answer, Mazy stopped swirling the color cream in the ceramic bowl. "You have a gown to wear tonight, right?"

"Yes."

"What's wrong with it?" Mazy propped her hands on her hips. "I can tell by your droopy mouth that you're not thrilled with the gown."

Droopy mouth? Sara made a conscious effort to smile. "I like it just fine." The olive-green ruffled sheath had been the only one in her size on the clearance rack at Dillard's. She hadn't even bothered trying it on, because she knew she'd hate it. But the price fit her budget, so she'd bought the dress. As soon as she returned from the ball, the garment was going into the Goodwill bag sitting in the hall closet.

Mazy sectioned off clumps of Sara's hair, then used a small paintbrush to apply the dye before rolling the hair in a piece of foil.

"What do your brothers think of you going with Travis to the Oilmen's Ball?"

"Gabe left town after Thanksgiving and Cole doesn't know I was invited to the ball." Travis had yet to bring her an official bid from Dominick, and until he did, she refused to discuss anything related to the Cartwright's with Cole. She hated to get her brother's hopes up that they'd come to an agreement with Dominick that would save the Bar T.

The morning passed quickly. Mazy colored, cut and styled Sara's hair, then gave her a makeover. "What do you think?" Mazy spun the chair to face the mirror.

The woman staring back at her was a stranger. Her hair was pinned up in a messy bob that was both sexy and sophisticated. The blond highlights framing her face made her appear younger than her thirty years. "What kind of makeup did you use?" Sara was afraid to touch her skin for fear she'd smudge the blush.

"Mineral powders. It's the latest craze."

Dark blue eyeliner and a light pink shadow accentuated the size and shape of Sara's brown eyes. Rose-colored lipstick made her mouth appear fuller. She wondered if Travis would be tempted to kiss her again.

"Take this with you." Mazy held out a sample-size tube of lipstick. "Peach might go better with your dress."

"Thank you."

Mazy grasped Sara's hands. "Do you have time for a manicure? Won't take but a minute to put nail tips on your fingers."

Sara grimaced at the hangnails and calluses. "Sure."

Mazy spent a half hour on Sara's hands, then glued half-moon tips to the end of her nails and painted them in a French manicure. "Much better. What about your toenails."

"I'm wearing close-toed shoes." She didn't own a pair of strappy high heels.

"Do you intend to wear shoes in bed with Travis, too?"

Face flushing, Sara stuttered. "I'm not... We're not..."

"Slip off your socks and shoes. I'd give you a bikini wax but—" Mazy checked her watch "—Doris asked if I could squeeze her in for a haircut after your appointment."

Doris got her haircut once a week so she could keep up on the local gossip. News of Sara attending the ball with Travis would be all over town by noon today.

Mazy made quick work of painting Sara's toenails, then used a handheld fan to dry the polish before applying a top coat. "Done." She dug through a wicker basket on the porch and produced a pair of flip-flops, then slid them on Sara's size-ten feet, leaving her heel hanging off the back. "Don't put shoes or nylons on for a couple of hours."

"I love my hair and the nails are perfect." Sara admired the tiny white flowers Mazy had drawn on each toenail, then she removed her wallet from her purse.

"This one's on me," Mazy said. "Neither of us has had a date in eons."

"At least let me leave a tip." Sara set two twenties on the counter.

Before she opened the door, Mazy said, "Hey, Sara."

"What?"

"If you get the chance, have wild, crazy sex with Travis tonight so I can live vicariously through you."

The outlandish comment replayed in Sara's mind all the way home. Back in her bedroom she decided to try her gown on to see which lipstick went better with the olive-green. The fit was a little tight. When she tugged hard to close the zipper in the back of the dress, the sharp sound of material tearing echoed through the room.

She spun in front of the mirror and gasped. The material had torn away from the zipper. Now what? She had three hours before Travis arrived. She picked up the phone and dialed a friend and fellow schoolteacher.

Kathy arrived at Sara's house ten minutes later and pronounced, "It's ruined." She studied the torn material. "The rip is too large. People will notice if you try to sew the ends of the material together."

"What am I going to do? There's no time to buy another dress." Sara felt a migraine coming on.

"Go have a glass of wine while I make a few calls."

Fighting tears, Sara left the room and headed for the kitchen. She'd guzzled half the wine in her glass when Kathy entered the room. "Okay, here's the plan. Beulah's going to let you borrow one of her mother's dresses."

"Beulah's mother was a prostitute."

"No, Viola was a madam."

Madam, prostitute—what's the difference? "I can't."

"Do you have a better plan?" Kathy quirked an eyebrow.

No.

"Viola was one of the most respected madams back in the day, and rumor has it, her dresses were the envy of every madam west of the Mississippi."

Oh, brother.

"At least go out to Beulah's and look at the gowns," Kathy said.

What other choice did Sara have? There was no time to drive into Tulsa to shop and there was no one her size in town to borrow a dress from. "Fine. I'll head over there now."

Kathy walked to the front door. "Let me know how things go."

Fifteen minutes later, Sara entered the pink Victorian and Beulah met her in the foyer. "Wow. Mazy did a heck of a job on your hair and makeup."

"Maybe now isn't a good time to try on dresses." Sara noticed the place was packed.

"Don't worry about the customers. They're too busy shoveling food into their mouths to pay attention to us." Beulah escorted Sara to the second floor—her private living quarters. "I set out Mama's prettiest dresses. Try one on, then come to the top of the stairs and call for me." Beulah opened a door at the end of the hall and ushered Sara into the turret room.

Decorated in pink and black, the walls were covered in fabric wallpaper—pink background with a black velvet fleur-de-lis pattern. Pink and black feather boas hung from crystal doorknobs mounted on the wall. Antique hat and shoe boxes littered the floor, and three gowns lay across the black satin comforter on the four-poster bed.

"They're stunning." Sara fingered a crystal bead on the sapphire-blue gown.

"Mama had style. Holler when you're ready." Beulah left, closing the door behind her.

All three dresses appealed to Sara, but she selected the least-revealing dress to try on first. The burgundy off-the-shoulder gown had two draped panels of black lace across the front of the skirt and a huge bow with black lace accents covering the bodice. The dress was suggestive yet elegant.

The dress, however, was a bit tight around the waist and she feared she'd pass out if she had to suck in her stomach the entire night. Maybe Beulah had a girdle she could borrow. The narrow skirt made long strides impossible, so she waddled like a duck to the top of the stairs. She hesitated calling Beulah's name, hoping to catch the woman as she passed through the foyer. No such luck. Sheriff's Deputy Ronny Dunlap noticed her and let out a wolf whistle.

"Is that you, Sara Sanders?" He grinned. "That dress suggests you're participating in an activity I might have to arrest you for."

"Go on with you now and leave Sara alone." Beulah paused at the foot of the stairs. She eyed the dress, then shook her head. "Nope. Try the next one."

Sara returned to the bedroom, where she put on the gold-and-brown gown with a full skirt, pleated bodice and a stylish twist at the waist. When she practiced walking around the room, she noticed the hem of the skirt ended an inch above the top of her foot. She'd have to wear flats with this dress.

When Sara returned to the stairs the foyer was packed with men.

"Hey, sweet thing, you can be my date tonight!" a voice in the crowd called out.

"I saw her first," the deputy shouted.

Beulah pushed her way through the men. "Twirl around." Sara obeyed. "Nope." Beulah shook her head. "Try the last one on."

Face flaming, Sara retreated to the turret room and studied the sapphire-blue gown that screamed *siren*. The dress was by far the sexiest of the three and one a schoolteacher would never buy in a million years.

Tonight you're not a teacher—you're Travis's date.

Made of silk taffeta the gown cinched at the waist. Silver rhinestones dangled from the plunging V-neck halter, which pushed Sara's breasts together, creating eye-popping cleavage. She shoved her girlfriends every which way but there was no making them less conspicuous. The flowing skirt draped gently over her hips and swirled around her legs when she walked.

Taking a deep breath, she left the room.

Dead silence greeted her at the top of the stairs.

"No?" she whispered, studying the slack-jawed gapes in the foyer.

Seconds ticked by, then a resounding "Yes!" exploded from the group.

"That's the one," Beulah said. "There's a pair of shoes dyed the exact color of the dress. Wear them, even if they hurt your feet." Beulah turned to her customers. "You morons quit gawking and go back to your tables."

Grinning like a brainy teenage girl who'd been asked to the prom by the quarterback of the football team, Sara returned to the bedroom and spun in a circle in front of the mirror. Hopefully the dress would have the same effect on Travis as it had had on the *morons*.

"How come I can't go?" Charlie sat on the bathroom counter watching Travis shave for the Oilmen's Christmas Ball.

"The dance is for adults only and it won't end until

way past your bedtime." He stroked the razor along his cheek, removing the last bit of shaving cream, then he wiped his face with a damp towel.

"I like to dance."

Since when? "Remember the dance lessons you had a few years ago?"

Charlie nodded.

"Grandma took you to three sessions, then you quit."

"The pink tights itched me." She wrinkled her nose. "What's Ms. Sanders gonna wear?"

"A pretty dress." Travis ignored the nervous twinge gripping his gut at the idea of dancing a waltz, fox-trot or the box step.

"Does Ms. Sanders like to dance?"

Travis slipped on his dress shirt, buttoned it, then tucked the tails into his pants. "I don't know." Maybe Sara had a pair of left feet, too. He'd prefer to hold her close and sway in one spot to the music.

"Dad?"

"What?" He rummaged through the vanity drawer, searching for the single bottle of cologne he owned.

"After the dance, are you gonna marry Ms. Sanders?"

The bottle slipped from his grip and banged against the counter. Luckily it didn't break. "What makes you ask that question?"

Solemn blue eyes studied him. "I think I want a mommy now."

Feeling as if he'd been whacked across the back of his head with a two-by-four, Travis was too stunned to respond.

"I didn't want a mommy when Grandma Charlotte was alive but…"

He tweaked Charlie's ponytail, hoping to tease the sadness from her eyes. "But what?"

"I miss Grandma." Charlie's lower lip wobbled.

"I know, honey." Travis hugged his daughter. "How would you like to tag along with me when I check on an oil derrick near Muskogee on Monday?"

Charlie's nose curled. Okay, so she wasn't keen on riding around in the truck with him all day. "I'll ask Aunt Sam if you can hang out at her house on Monday." Samantha had invited Charlie over to play with Luke anytime during the kids' winter break.

"I like Luke. He's really smart."

Sara had told Travis that the boy's I.Q. was near genius.

Changing the subject, Charlie said, "If you married Ms. Sanders, I could live with her and then Juanita wouldn't have to watch me when you go to work or Grandpa flies out of town."

The past week Travis had done a lot of thinking while driving from one derrick to the next. He'd believed it would take time to determine if he and Charlie belonged in Tulapoint, but with each passing day he was more convinced this is where they were meant to be.

He hadn't expected to like working on the mainland as much as he did. He had trouble picturing himself back on the Hoover Diana. Travis wasn't under any illusions that he and Dominick would always see eye-to-eye on work-related issues or personal matters, but with time Travis hoped they'd develop a mutual respect and affection for one another.

Think about what's best for Charlie. He might be

away from his daughter during the day but he enjoyed coming home at night and spending time with her. If he returned to his old job, then Charlie would need a full-time nanny and he wanted to do better by his daughter.

Travis wasn't an overly emotional guy. If he'd worn his feelings on his sleeve while working on an ocean rig, he'd have had been laughed right off the platform. Still, he admitted Sara made him feel things a rough-neck shouldn't—tenderness. Compassion.

Sara was independent. Sensible. She had a fulfilling career and didn't need a man to take care of her. And she was loyal to those she loved. If he and Charlie made Tulapoint their permanent home, then his friendship with Sara would continue to grow.

"Dad?" Charlie tugged his sleeve.

"What?"

"Do you like Ms. Sanders?"

"Yes, I do, Charlie. She's a nice lady."

"Does Ms. Sanders like you?"

"I believe she does." Travis was eager to convince Sara to sell Dominick the drilling rights to the Bar T, then the way would be cleared for him and Sara to focus on their personal relationship.

"If you marry Ms. Sanders, will I get a brother or sister to play with?"

"Don't get ahead of yourself, kiddo. Sara and I are just friends."

At the sound of a car door slamming, Charlie hopped to the floor. "That's Juanita. She said Luke and I can stay up late and watch a movie." His daughter's shoes clunked against the steps as she raced downstairs to meet the housekeeper.

Earlier in the week, Samantha had suggested that Luke and Charlie have a sleepover the night of the ball, since she and Wade planned to attend the party, too. Juanita had agreed to bring Luke out to the Lazy River and spend the night with the kids.

Travis finished dressing, said his goodbyes to the kids and headed into Tulapoint. Less than a half hour later, he parked in front of Sara's house and donned the black cowboy hat he'd purchased for the occasion. He checked his watch—ten minutes early. He climbed the front steps, then paced the length of the porch. Though he anticipated seeing Sara in an evening gown, part of him wished they were heading to a drive-in movie. Not even his Armani tux made Travis feel as if he belonged with the wealthy crowd.

The curtains in the front window fluttered. *Walter.* The ugly cat sat on the windowsill, stubby tail twitching as he gave Travis a one-eyed evil glare.

Don't worry, bad boy. I won't hurt your mama.

A movement in the room behind Walter caught Travis's attention. *Holy smokes.* A vision of stunning perfection waltzed through the foyer. Nose pressed to the windowpane, Travis watched Sara apply her lipstick in the hall mirror. Arousal shot through him when she pursed her lips in a fake kiss. Sara's transformation from small-town schoolteacher to goddess stirred his blood. Before she caught him ogling, he rang the bell.

Sara opened the door. "Hello, Travis."

Good God. Where did all that cleavage come from? He couldn't find the strength to look away from the silver rhinestones dangling off the bodice. "Wow."

"You like the dress?"

He shoved his hands into his trouser pockets to keep

from fingering one of the dangling jewels. "You're stunning, Sara."

"Thank you." She smiled. "I like your hat."

"We'd better hit the road." Or else he'd give in to temptation and behave like a true roughneck—toss Sara over his shoulder, haul her up to the bedroom and have his way with her.

When Sara stepped from the house and turned to lock the door, a whiff of perfume floated beneath his nose and he leaned in to nuzzle the back of her neck. "You smell nice."

"Thank you." The words escaped in a soft sigh.

"You should wear high heels more often," he said when she faced him.

"Why?"

"Easier to kiss you."

Chapter Nine

Once Travis and Sara were on the road to Tulsa, he turned on the radio. Country music filled the cab as he concentrated on corralling his wayward hormones. At the moment he was incapable of conversation—all his senses acutely attuned to the woman riding in the front seat with him. Sara's dress was made to seduce a man and it was doing a heck of a job on him.

Up until now his feelings for Sara had been mostly platonic. He liked her. He thought she was smart. Funny. Loyal. Tonight, he'd add sexy and desirable to her list of admirable qualities. He'd believed the few kisses he'd shared with Sara had been the result of having gotten caught up in the proverbial moment with her—not anymore.

Damn, he hadn't seen this coming. He stared at her profile. He couldn't believe the transformation in her. He'd always considered her attractive in a girl-next-door way, but there was nothing plain about the woman sitting two feet from him. By the time they reached the outskirts of Tulsa, Travis had succeeded in convincing certain parts of his anatomy to behave like a gentleman.

When he drove down Brady Street, Sara asked, "Isn't the ball being held at the Crowne Plaza Hotel?"

"Samantha said they changed the venue this year to the Brady Theater. Something wrong with the theater?"

"No, it's wonderful. The building used to be called the Tulsa Convention Hall. It was built in the early 1900s. Back in the 1950s, the hotel went under a massive renovation."

"Thanks for the history lesson, teach." Travis grinned, yearning to pull her close and make history with her mouth. Instead, he parked outside the theater and a valet attendant opened the passenger-side door.

"Good evening." He helped Sara from the truck, then caught the keys when Travis tossed them across the hood.

"Enjoy the ball, sir." The attendant hopped into the truck and sped off.

Travis placed his hand against the curve of Sara's lower back and escorted her into the building. Camera flashes and instrumental music greeted them when they walked through the doors. Ignoring the curious stares of the partygoers, they joined the reception line, where his father and several members of Cartwright Oil's board of directors greeted guests.

"I hope your father doesn't make a scene when he sees me," she said.

"If anyone is making a scene, it's you in that dress." Travis noticed several men stare at Sara. He slid his arm around her waist and whispered in her ear. "I've never been the envy of every man in a room. Stop worrying and let me enjoy the moment."

"You're incorrigible."

"I know." When their turn came to greet the host, Sara spoke first. "Hello, Dominick."

"Sara." Dominick waved his hand toward the couples on the dance floor. "These kinds of social events could become commonplace for you if we can come to some sort of agreement about your ranch."

Sara ignored his father's comment, but it reminded Travis to keep his eye on the goal. He was so distracted by Sara tonight that business was the furthest thing from his mind.

Dominick turned to Travis. "I'd like to introduce you to my colleagues this evening."

"I won't be difficult to spot—find the most beautiful woman in the room and I'll be at her side." With a bounce in his step, Travis led Sara to the buffet table filled with lobster, crab puffs, fondues and exotic cheese and fruit sculptures.

Before they had a chance to fill their plates, an elderly woman grasped Travis's elbow. "Young man, I've been a friend of your father's since my daddy first struck oil in Arkansas." The elderly woman smiled at Sara. "You won't mind, dear, if I introduce Travis around?"

Sara searched the partygoers and found Dominick watching her. The oil baron had sent the old biddy to steal Travis away. Fine. She'd show Dominick she could hold her own with Tulsa's elite society. Sara nodded. "By all means, take him."

"But—"

"You know—" The older woman cut Travis off "—you're the spitting image of your father when he was younger."

Fearing she'd laugh, Sara pressed her lips together and ignored her date's pleading expression. "I want you to meet Patrice Gallwinger. Her great-granddaddy fought off the Osage Indians back in..."

As soon as they were out of earshot, Sara added a few hors d'oeuvres to her plate. She'd been too nervous to eat lunch before Travis had picked her up this evening, and she was famished. No sense allowing good food to go to waste. The moment she popped a crab puff in her mouth, a finger tapped her shoulder.

An older gentleman bowed. "Caught you with your mouth full, did I?"

Sara swallowed too quickly. The food lodged in her throat, cutting off her airway.

"Allow me." The gentleman snatched a champagne flute from the tray of a passing waiter.

She downed the drink in one gulp, then gasped, "Thank you."

His gaze roamed unapologetically over her body. "I don't imagine a beautiful woman such as you is here without a date."

Was the coot hitting on her? He was at least sixty-five—handsome yes, but old enough to be her father. "I came with Travis Cartwright. Dominick's—"

"Ah, yes. The black sheep of the family." He sipped his drink. "We were all shocked to learn Charlotte had kept Travis from his rightful place in the Cartwright empire."

Empire—oh, brother. "I'm afraid I didn't catch your name."

"Allow me to introduce myself." He held out his hand. "Benjamin Reynolds." Sara offered her hand and the geezer boldly kissed it.

"Nice to meet you, Mr. Reynolds."

"Benjamin. Please."

"Benjamin. I'm Sara Sanders. I teach second grade in Tulapoint in addition to being Dominick's arch enemy and royal pain in his arse."

"Well, it's a relief to discover I'm not the only thorn in Dominick's backside."

"Really? What have you done to get on his bad side?"

"I outbid him on a well a few years back and it turned out to be quite profitable."

"Well, that wasn't very nice."

He chuckled. "And you?"

"Dominick wants the oil on my family's ranch and is threatening me and my brothers with a bogus lawsuit."

"Doesn't sound like Dominick."

"What doesn't sound like me?" Dominick joined them, and Sara held her breath, wondering if she was about to be tossed out of the soiree on her head.

"Had I known you invited such visions of loveliness to your annual ball, I would have shown up at the event before now." Benjamin winked at Sara.

"This *vision*—" Dominick nodded to Sara "—happens to be my neighbor."

"Yes, I know. What's this I hear about you harassing her with a lawsuit?"

"I'm bidding top dollar for their property." Dominick's eyes narrowed.

Sara snatched a second flute of champagne from a waiter. She'd need a few drinks before the night was over. "What Mr. Cartwright refuses to acknowledge is that I made a promise to my father and—"

"You're father's dead." Dominick glared.

Sara gasped. "How dare—"

"No, young lady. How dare your father."

Stunned, Sara watched Dominick walk off and join a group of conversing men. What in the world did Dominick have against her father?

Benjamin nodded toward the dance floor. "Shall we?"

"We shall." Sara allowed Benjamin to twirl her around, but after two songs the codger became bold and slid his hand over her fanny. "Oh, no," she said, placing his fingers against the small of her back.

Benjamin threw his head back and laughed. "Can't blame an old man for trying."

"You're very charming, Benjamin. Why aren't you married?"

"I've made the infamous trip down the aisle four times."

"And none of your marriages has worked out?"

"Bit of a problem with infidelity." He shrugged. "I bore easily."

The song ended, but Benjamin tightened his hold on her waist and continued dancing. "Have you retained a lawyer to protect you from Dominick's threats?"

"My brothers and I can't afford a lawyer," Sara answered honestly. "Even if I allow Cartwright Oil to drill on our property, I don't trust Dominick not to keep harassing us until he owns our ranch lock, stock and barrel."

A gentleman tapped Benjamin's shoulder. "May I cut in?"

"Good evening, Howard." Benjamin bowed. "May I present Sara Sanders. Sara, Howard Barker. He owns Tulsa Savings and Loan."

"And five other banks." Howard bowed. She could get used to old-fashioned gallantry.

"Pleasure to meet you, Howard."

Benjamin transferred Sara's hand to her new dance partner's, then warned, "Mind your manners, Howard. Sara's a schoolteacher."

"Schoolteacher?" Howard's eyes rounded. "I thought you were a...a..."

Sara smiled. "A what?"

Howard leaned in and whispered, "An escort, my dear."

A hooker?

"I recognized your dress. Viola wore that for me. It was a favorite of mine."

Howard had known Viola when she'd been a madam. "Didn't Viola eventually retire from the business?"

"Yes, but she continued to entertain a few select clients until shortly before she succumbed to a heart attack."

"How old are you, Howard?"

"Eighty-two." His expression turned dreamy. "Viola initiated me into manhood on my eighteenth birthday."

Sara blushed.

"I must say, you do the gown justice, dear."

"I promise you, I'm a schoolteacher. There was a problem with the original dress I bought for the ball and Beulah—" Sara waved a hand in the air. "Never mind."

"I'm not the only gentleman here who recognized Viola's dress."

Oh, dear. "Dominick isn't one of them, is he?"

"No. Dominick was a child when Viola bought

the old Victorian and had it painted that awful pink."
Howard motioned to Travis and the ever-growing circle
of females surrounding him. "Are you and Travis…"

"Friends. His daughter is a student in my class."

"Friends you say?" Howard pulled her closer. "Let's
see if we can make him jealous."

Sara didn't know whether to stomp on the old man's
foot or laugh. "Are you married, Howard?"

"I'm a widower." He dipped Sara low—so low her
breasts threatened to spill from the gown.

"Here he comes. Now, play along, dear." Howard
pulled Sara upright.

"Pardon me." Travis's voice carried over Sara's
shoulder.

Howard swung her the opposite way. Travis followed
them across the floor. "May I cut in?"

"Not now, son. Can't an old man live out his
fantasy?"

Travis continued to stalk them. "You've had my date
as your dance partner for the past three songs."

"Keeping count, are we, young man?"

Sara swallowed a giggle.

"Damn right, I'm keeping count. Now, give her back
before—"

"Before what? Are you challenging me to a fist-
fight?"

"Oh, for God's sake," Travis grumbled.

"All right, you two. Enough is enough." Sara pulled
away from Howard. "Travis, this is Howard—"

"I know, the man who owns all the banks." Travis
scowled. "My father told me to be nice to you."

Howard hooted. "Dominick has his hands full with

you." Howard nodded to Sara. "Don't let her get away. She's a gem."

Travis crushed Sara against him, forcing the air from her lungs.

My, oh my. She could get used men fighting over her.

TRAVIS TWIRLED SARA through the throng of dancers. He yearned to take her somewhere—preferably a hotel room—where he could ditch his tux and gentlemanly manners. "Are you ready to blow this party?"

"What will your father say if we cut out early?"

"Nothing. I've met all the important people on his list, so the rest of the evening is mine to do with as I please."

Sara's wistful expression as she looked around reminded Travis that his date had few chances to attend fancy balls. "Unless you want to stay," he added. For Sara, he'd suffer through another few hours of socializing with the rich, famous and annoying.

Her brown eyes darkened and the corner of her mouth tilted in a come-hither smile. "I'm ready to leave."

His pulse accelerated, pumping blood through his veins at breakneck speed. "Good. Your evening gown has endeared you to every man in this room." He softly nipped her neck, and she shivered. "But I'm the lucky guy who gets to take you home."

When the song ended, Travis led Sara off the dance floor, but Dominick thwarted their escape. "You're not leaving, are you?"

"Sara and I are heading back to Tulapoint," Travis said.

Dominick motioned to the women gathered near the

buffet table. "Your sister and Wade arrived over an hour ago and she's been waiting for a chance to speak with you."

Travis hadn't noticed Samantha or her husband— he'd been too busy keeping track of Sara and her lecherous fan club. Right then, his sister waved. Travis made a gesture with his hand that he'd phone her later.

"I hope to hear from you soon, Sara." Dominick's eyes narrowed.

"I'll need an official offer before I agree to discuss anything with you."

"You'll have the paperwork within twenty-four hours."

"This isn't the time or place." Travis leveled his best back-off glare at his father. He respected Dominick's business acumen, work ethic and general devotion to family, but his father didn't know when to quit pushing his agenda.

After a strained silence, Dominick said, "I trust you both enjoyed yourselves tonight."

"Very much, thank you," Sara said.

"Drive safely." Dominick walked off to join the men at the bar.

As soon as Travis and Sara stepped outside the theater, the valet attendant brought the truck around to the front. Travis helped Sara into the cab, then sped off. He'd driven three blocks when Sara exhaled loudly. Worried his father had ruined his chances of prolonging their evening together, he asked, "What's wrong?"

"Nothing. I loved every minute of tonight."

"So you enjoy being accosted by old men and receiving evil-eyed glares from their prudish wives?"

Smiling, she closed her eyes. "Tonight was just about perfect."

Tonight wasn't over. He stopped at a red light, leaned across the seat and kissed Sara.

"Mmm..." Her throaty sound encouraged him and he nibbled a path down her neck.

A horn honked behind them. "Light's green," she whispered.

Travis hit the gas too hard and the truck lurched forward. "Sorry." He grasped her hand and pressed her fingers against his thigh. He left downtown Tulsa behind and merged onto the highway. Even though she'd dressed like a siren for the ball, Travis guessed Sara was anything *but* experienced with men. He was glad and worried at the same time.

Sara fidgeted in her seat.

"What's wrong?" Travis asked.

"Nothing, it's just that...I'm not sure what you're expecting from me once we reach my house."

Sara was thinking along the same lines he'd been thinking all night—sex.

Her fingers dug into his thigh muscle. "You're going over the speed limit." The speedometer needle edged toward eighty.

He eased up on the accelerator. All this thinking about sex distracted him. He and Julie had never discussed having sex the first time they'd slept together—it had just happened.

Sara's not Julie.

Even though Travis's attraction to Sara was more than physical, they hadn't known each other long. "No matter what happens or doesn't happen between us tonight—" he kissed her fingertips "—I want you to know that I'm crazy about you."

"Crazy?"

"You're fun to be with. You're smart. Loyal. Nice." He grinned. "Sexy."

"It's the dress."

"No. It's you." Travis gripped the steering wheel tighter. "You have no idea how badly I want to pull over and take that dress off you."

Sara's breath rushed from her mouth. "As interesting as roadside sex sounds, I'd hate to ruin Viola's gown."

"Who's Viola?"

"Beulah's mother."

He eyed Sara's cleavage. "Beulah's mother must be a hell of a knockout if she still wears dresses like that."

"Beulah's mother passed away years ago, but in her glory days she was a madam."

"You don't say?"

"Those lecherous men you accused me of teasing tonight…"

"What about them?" he asked.

"They recognized the dress."

"Brought back fond memories for the geezers, eh?" Travis chuckled.

Sara worried her lower lip. "Maybe it's not such a good idea to…"

"Sleep together," he said.

"Until your father and I resolve our differences."

"Our relationship has nothing to do with my father," Travis insisted. And he meant it. Yes, Travis wanted to win his father's approval by helping to negotiate a business deal between him and Sara, but if that didn't pan out, Travis still intended to continue seeing Sara.

"Dominick brought up the past tonight, but as usual he neglected to say what my father did that was so unforgivable."

"Was your dad one of the few men in Oklahoma who refused to sell out to Dominick?"

"I don't think that's it. You should have seen the expression in your father's eyes. It was hurt, not anger." She shifted toward Travis. "I'm beginning to suspect Dominick's obsession with owning the Bar T has nothing at all to do with oil."

"Don't allow my father to get inside your head." Travis took the exit ramp off the interstate. They were ten minutes from Tulapoint, and damned if he wasn't going to give it his best shot to reclaim the romantic mood.

"Our being together might adversely affect Charlie. She's still adjusting to the loss of her grandmother, a new home, a new family and school. She doesn't need any additional strife in her life."

"Charlie's doing great—because of you. Any time I spend with you is a positive thing." He didn't want to scare Sara off by telling her about earlier this evening when Charlie had declared that she was ready for a new mother.

"I worry Charlie will get her hopes up that something will come of us seeing each other," Sara said.

"My daughter's a tough little girl."

"What if our relationship affects how your father treats Charlie? She adores Dominick and talks about him all the time at school. I don't want to come between the two of them."

"That won't happen, promise." Travis got the feeling Sara was using Dominick and Charlie as excuses and wished he understood the real reason she hesitated taking their relationship to the next level.

He slowed the truck when they reached the town limits. A block later, he parked in front of Sara's Victorian. At one in the morning, the streetlamp cast an eerie glow across the sidewalk.

"Ask me to stay," he said.

Her smile sent a jolt through his body. "Stay," she whispered.

"You won't be sorry." He leaned across the seat and kissed her—slow and easy. She threaded her fingers through his hair, convincing him with her mouth that she wanted him—at least for tonight.

"Mmm." He drew his thumb across her lower lip. "Where does a schoolteacher learn to kiss like that?"

"She doesn't. You bring out the wild side in me."

"If it's wild you want, it's wild you'll get, sweetheart." He hurried to the other side of the truck and helped her out. They climbed the porch steps, stopping three times to kiss before entering the house. Travis backed Sara toward the stairs, but she put on the brakes.

I must be crazy. Sara stared at her and Travis's reflection in the hall mirror. Viola's dress made her feel beautiful and desirable—but would she feel that way once the dress came off? Or would Travis see the country girl everyone in town saw.

Her gaze collided with Travis's in the mirror and the heat in his eyes reassured her.

He slid a finger beneath her dress strap and moved it aside, then kissed her shoulder. She shivered at the feel of his lips on her skin, dreaming of all the places his mouth would explore before the evening ended.

"What are you afraid of?" he asked.

"Nothing." *Everything.* She pressed herself against him. Women like her didn't go to bed with men like Travis. He was out of her league—at least, in the bedroom. Her sexual experience was limited—how on earth would she satisfy him? She didn't even know where to begin.

He brushed aside a strand of hair clinging to her cheek. "Fess up, Sara Sanders, because when I get you upstairs, there's not going to be any room in that bed for doubts." Travis backed her across the foyer one step at a time, stopping every other second to kiss her.

At the top of the stairs, she trailed her fingertip across his lower lip. *Just once, take what you want and to heck with the consequences. If this is all you and Travis ever have, then grab it and run.*

Sara was a grown woman—mature enough to handle a one-night stand or two or three before Travis came to his senses and figured out she wasn't his type.

Before she lost her courage, she grasped his hand and led him into her bedroom.

Chapter Ten

Travis lay on his side, spooning Sara in her queen-size bed. Twice hadn't been enough—he wanted her again. He cupped her warm breast and buried his face in her sweet-smelling hair. Making love to Sara had been incredible. More than he'd imagined. More than he'd dared dream. They'd connected—not just their bodies, but their souls. And hearts.

His caresses stirred Sara awake. Eyes closed, she stretched on her back, one side of her mouth curving into a lazy smile. The light from the full moon spilled across the bed, casting a warm glow over her face. His loving had left her lips swollen, hair mussed and eyeliner smudged. She looked wanton and witchy—not the least bit like a teacher.

Discovering their compatibility in the bedroom forced Travis to acknowledge that friendship with Sara was out of the question. No one was more surprised than him that his goal of getting to know Sara in order to win points with his father would turn into something bigger than he could have imagined. Sara rocked his world with her gentle touches, passionate kisses and whispered words of encouragement. Shy and hesitant, then bold and sassy, she'd tied his heartstrings into one giant knot.

"I know you're awake." He nibbled her ear.

"Again?" She groaned, then giggled, when he tickled her side.

"Tired of me already?" Kisses accompanied his question.

"Never." Curling her hand around his neck, Sara urged him closer. Travis obliged, happy to allow her to do all the work—and man, did she put in the overtime. A few minutes later, they lay panting, staring at the ceiling.

"I think this makes us officially *more* than friends now," he said.

Sara stiffened at Travis's declaration. She rolled onto her side—their faces inches apart on the pillow. He was so darned handsome. How long had she dreamed of finding a man to spend the rest of her life with? Build a future with. Raise a family with. Everything inside her yearned to take a chance on Travis, but she'd learned the hard way not to trust impassioned speeches and declarations of love.

Travis hasn't said he loves you. Dare she hope the warm heat in his dark brown eyes signaled his feelings for her were sincere?

"Why the worried frown?" He brushed his fingertip across her cheek.

Sara forced a smile. If she could go back in time to when she'd first seen Travis and Charlie at Beulah's, she'd never have allowed Travis to slip past her defenses. She'd have kept her guard up around the roughneck. *Too late now.* She cared for Travis, but feared in the light of day he'd realize his feelings for her had been the result of getting caught up in the moment—the Oilmen's Ball, her sexy gown. The next time Travis saw her, she'd be Sara the schoolteacher, not Sara the siren.

Throat aching, she drowned in Travis's dark eyes. She wanted to give him a chance to prove his intentions were honest and true. But that would mean spending more time with him and she couldn't hold him at bay that long. It wouldn't take much effort on Travis's part to coax her heart to fall in love with him.

He kissed her ear, then her cheek, then her chin. "Talk to me, Sara."

Gathering her courage, she said, "This...probably wasn't a good idea." His eyes widened as if she'd slapped him. "I think we should just stay friends." Friends was not what she wanted, but it was safe.

"I know we haven't known each other long, but we're not young teenagers. We're mature adults who've been knocked around by life." He pressed a finger to her lips, halting her objection. "I admit, it seems too soon for a serious relationship, but you make me happy. I want to be with you."

She'd known Josh one week when he'd begun his campaign to win her over. Josh had pursued her relentlessly, and when she'd insisted on slowing things down, he'd doubled his efforts and had won her over with false declarations of love and flowers. The jerk had even written her a poem.

"There have been lots of changes in your life lately and—"

"I'm not using you as a crutch, Sara." His mouth covered hers in a kiss that scattered her thoughts and common sense.

When she regained her cognitive powers, she asked, "What about Dominick?"

"My father has no say in my personal life. If you decide to negotiate a drilling lease with my father, I'll make sure he treats you and your brothers fairly."

Travis wouldn't allow Dominick to take advantage of their relationship, but she hated to be a source of stress between the two men, especially when Travis was trying to fit in with his new family.

More kisses. More caresses. More scattered thoughts.

His brown eyes clung to hers, their warmth hugging her soul. "Promise me that you'll think about giving us a chance," he said.

"Promise." She doubted her mind would contemplate much else for the foreseeable future.

SHOES IN HAND, TRAVIS snuck through the back door at four in the morning. He made it halfway across the dark kitchen before Dominick's words stopped him cold.

"I've been waiting for you."

"You scared the hell out of me." Travis hadn't noticed his father sitting at the table. He flipped on the light and the old man squinted.

"Where were you?"

Beaming, Travis said. "The last time anyone waited up for me, I was sixteen. I'd just gotten my driver's license and Mom worried that I'd crashed her car and she wouldn't have a way to get to work the next morning." Feeling foolish for carrying his shoes, Travis set them on the floor, then grabbed a water bottle from the fridge. Making love to Sara had been an exercise in endurance.

"What's going on between you and Sara?" his father asked.

"I like Sara. A lot. She makes me happy and Charlie adores her."

"You didn't propose to her tonight, did you?"

"No, but—"

"You just met her a few weeks ago."

"How long did you know my mother before you became serious about her?"

"Never mind about your mother." Dominick shoved a hand through his hair. "If you're smart, you'll stick to business where Sara Sanders is concerned."

No sense arguing with his father. It would take time for both Dominick and Sara to accept that Travis's feelings for her were serious. He understood and sympathized with Sara's reservations—the fact they hadn't known each other long. And he hadn't forgotten that Sara had been burned in the past by another man. And there was always the unfinished business between the Bar T and Cartwright Oil hanging over their heads. Even so, Travis was determined to prove his intentions toward Sara were honest and heartfelt.

Lest his father devise a plan to sabotage his efforts, Travis warned, "My relationship with Sara is no one's business but mine."

"You'd betray your own flesh and blood?"

"Betray?" Travis shoved his chair away from the table and paced in front of the back door. He'd been the one betrayed by his mother and father. "I don't know what happened between you and Mom, but I wonder if she took off because you were too controlling."

Dominick stared in shock, but Travis felt no sympathy. He was tired of his father's uncompromising attitude. "Maybe my mother played a role in the breakup of your marriage, but if you bullied her the way you're bullying me, the way you've bullied Sara and her brothers, then me and my mother were better off without you."

As soon as the words left his mouth, Travis wished to call them back. Dominick's wide-eyed stare hit Travis square in the gut. He was no better than his father, tossing around threats. "Sorry. I shouldn't have said that."

"You don't know what you're talking about, son."

"Then tell me—why did Mom leave you?"

Dominick stared into space as seconds ticked off the wall clock. "Charlotte had an affair."

The air rushed from Travis's lungs, leaving him winded and dizzy. He'd always believed his mother had chosen to raise him alone to protect him from a father who hadn't wanted him. To learn he'd been denied a family because of his mother's own selfish agenda was like a hot poker in the eye. Travis struggled to accept that the loving mother he'd known all his life had been at fault for the demise of his parent's marriage and breakup of the family. How could he forgive her for purposefully keeping him from his father and siblings?

For the first time since arriving at the Lazy River, Travis felt sorry for his father. "Are you sure?"

"She told me she was in love with another man and no longer wanted to be married to me."

That must have been a deadly blow to a man as prideful as Dominick. To learn his mother—not his father—had betrayed their marriage vows bewildered Travis. The hurt little boy in him asked, "You two couldn't have worked out your problems?"

"Your mother never gave me the chance. She packed her bags and left."

Not only had Dominick's wife walked out on him for another man, she'd also left her children behind. Travis wondered if his mother had tried to redeem herself through the years by helping Travis raise Charlie.

"After your mother took off, Jake Sanders showed up drunk on the doorstep one evening."

Sara's father?

Dominick clenched his hands into fists—a testament to the anger his father still harbored over the past. "Sanders confessed that he'd been sleeping with Charlotte right under my nose."

Travis collapsed on a chair and stared into space. His mother and Sara's father...?

"Charlotte and Sanders had intended to run off together, but their plans developed a kink when Mary Sanders discovered she was pregnant with Sara."

Jake hadn't had the heart to leave a pregnant wife, but Travis's mother hadn't been bothered by the idea of leaving behind two young children. "All those years my mother was waiting for Jake Sanders to come for her." Travis found the story incredulous and sad.

"After six months passed, I hired a detective to locate Charlotte—as much as I despised her for cheating on me, I needed to know that she was okay. And Sam and Matt kept asking when their mother was coming home." Dominick's voice wavered. Even grumpy old men weren't immune to heartbreak.

"The private eye located Charlotte in Houston, where she was working as a secretary for a car dealership. That's when I learned she was pregnant."

"You thought the baby belonged to Sanders."

"Damn straight I did. My lawyer hand delivered the divorce papers the next week. I think when Charlotte realized Jake had no intention of leaving Mary for her, she purposefully kept you a secret from me. She knew that if I learned you were my son, I'd sue for custody and she'd be left alone." Dominick tapped his finger against the tabletop. "I want to make it perfectly clear...I would have taken you away from Charlotte if I'd known you were mine. You should have been raised a Cartwright from the beginning."

"Are Sara and her brothers aware of the affair?" Travis asked.

"I don't know."

"Have you told Matt and Sam?"

A lengthy silence filled the kitchen. "Matt knows his mother had an affair, but not with who. Neither of us has told Sam. She'd just get upset over and over again when the subject came up, because she'd have forgotten she'd been told before."

Matt hadn't mentioned their mother's affair. Maybe he'd assumed Travis already knew.

"I understand why you had a grudge against Jake all these years, but he's dead now. You can't hold Sara and her brothers responsible for their father's actions."

"I don't hold them responsible."

"Then why is it so important for you to have their ranch? Don't you have enough oil in all your other wells? When is enough money enough? A hundred million? Two hundred million? A billion?"

"It's never been about the money."

"Then what is it about?"

"I lost a wife and I lost all those years with you

because Sanders couldn't keep his pants zipped. He owes me."

Travis had more questions for his father, but Dominick shoved his chair back and stood. "I'll phone Sara with an official bid tomorrow morning." He grabbed his car keys from the counter and walked out the back door.

Emotionally drained, Travis watched the taillights of his father's old Chevy Apache pickup disappear. He thought of his mother's selfishness—sacrificing what was best for her family in hopes of winning her heart's desire. He thought about Jake Sanders—he'd forsaken his marriage vows and torn apart another man's family. And Dominick was no better than his wife and neighbor—unable to let go of the past, he sought revenge against a dead man's children.

Now that Travis had reconnected with his father and siblings, he wanted a lasting relationship with his new family, but if Dominick couldn't accept that Travis had feelings for Sara, then he wouldn't be a part of Travis's and Charlie's lives.

"Coffee?"

Startled, Travis jumped inside his skin. He hadn't heard Juanita enter the room. "Sure." After his talk with Dominick, Travis was wide-awake anyway.

"Don't be hard on your father," she said.

"You heard our conversation?"

"I'm an old woman. I sleep in snatches." She pointed to the laundry room. "When I don't sleep, I work."

Travis returned to the table and sat.

"Your father loved your mother very much," Juanita said. "But Charlotte did not love him the same way."

That didn't excuse his mother's actions. "Do you know where Dominick went just now?"

"To the cabin."

"What cabin?" Dominick had given Travis a tour of the ranch the day after Thanksgiving, but they'd never come across a cabin.

"The cabin where your mother and Jake Sanders met in secret." Juanita carried two mugs of coffee to the table and joined Travis.

Travis couldn't imagine the hurt and anger his father must have felt at his wife's betrayal.

"Charlotte taught your father a valuable lesson."

"What's that?"

"Money and power will never win over true love."

"I'm grateful to you for telling me this, Juanita."

"Your father's a good man."

His father had been wronged by his wife and neighbor, but until Dominick let go of the past, there would be no happiness for the Cartwrights and the Sanderses.

"'MORNING, COLE." Sara entered the tack room in the barn early Monday morning.

Her brother perused her up and down. "A buddy of mine spotted a truck pulling away from your house at three-thirty in the morning yesterday."

Sara's face flushed and she cursed her embarrassment. She was a grown woman who had a right to her privacy—not that anyone in and around Tulapoint knew the definition of the word *privacy*. By now, the locals were buzzing with the news of Travis's late-night visit. "Did you send your friend to spy on me?"

"Hardly. Kenny's been dating the widow who lives down the block from you." Cole grinned. "He must have been sneaking out of her house the same time Travis was sneaking out of yours."

Sara swatted her brother's shoulder. "I didn't know Kenny was seeing Susie Cummings." Sara minded her own business, which meant she was the last one to find out the latest gossip.

"How was the Oilmen's Ball?"

"Lots of stuffed shirts and fancy food." She smiled at the memory of her dance partners. "Mostly old people."

"So, did you and Travis..." Cole waggled his eyebrows.

Her brother appeared insistent on sticking his nose where it didn't belong. "Mind your own business."

He grabbed a can of linseed oil from a shelf, unscrewed the cap, soaked a rag and went to work polishing a saddle. "You've got that look on your face."

"What look?"

"The look that says you did it."

She played dumb. "Did what?"

"The down'n'dirty with Cartwright."

She and Travis had *made love*, but she wasn't about to argue terminology with her brother. "I didn't drive all the way out here to discuss my sex life."

"So the schoolteacher got herself a little nookie, eh?"

"Knock it off. There's something serious I need to discuss with you."

His face sobered. "I'm listening."

There was no easy way to broach the subject, so she got right to the point. "What would you think if Travis and I began dating seriously?"

Her brother set aside the rag. "How seriously?"

"Very."

"Ah, you have *serious* feelings for Travis."

"Yes." She rubbed at an imaginary spot on her pants. "I'm scared and I don't want to get hurt again." What she felt for Travis didn't compare to what she'd felt for Josh.

"What makes you believe Travis will hurt you?"

Be honest. Cole had been the one to wipe her tears after Josh had trampled her heart. "I don't know what Travis sees in me. He could do a lot better than plain-looking me."

Several seconds passed before Cole spoke. "You have a lot to interest a man, Sara. Don't sell yourself short. You have a college degree. A steady job. You're independent and you own a home. And you've never shied away from hard work."

"Sounds like you're describing a man, not a woman." She shoved a hand through her hair. "Travis doesn't need a woman with a steady job. Or an education. Or one willing to work hard."

"What are you getting at?" Cole asked.

"Travis could get any woman he wanted. Why me?" Cole opened his mouth to speak, but she held up a hand. "And don't tell me I'm attractive—I hate that word. People use that word to describe someone who...who... looks like me. Plain."

"Beauty is in the eye of the beholder, sis. If Travis likes what he sees, who are you to argue with him?"

She worried that Travis might view her in a different light once the excitement of a new relationship wore off. Tears welled in her eyes and Cole pulled her close for a hug. "I know Josh hurt you real bad. But don't let what he did ruin the rest of your life. You're older.

Wiser. Trust your heart. Don't let Josh's betrayal keep you from finding happiness with another man."

"Thanks." Sara squeezed her brother's ribs.

"What about Travis's daughter? How will she react when she learns her teacher likes her father?"

"Charlie and I get along great. I don't think she'll mind in the least if Travis and I date."

"Does Dominick know Travis has feelings for you?"

"I doubt he'll approve, but Travis doesn't seem worried." She sniffed. "You never answered my question—how do *you* feel about me dating a Cartwright?"

"If Travis makes you happy, then see him all you want."

"Travis promised he'd make Dominick treat us fairly if we decide to do business with him."

"Are you considering a drilling lease with Cartwright Oil?"

If she and Travis were determined to give their relationship their all, then she had to mend fences with her neighbor. "Dominick phoned this morning with an offer."

"And…?"

"Ten thousand dollars per acre. He wants access to two hundred acres."

Cole whistled low. "That's two million a year in revenue."

And five times the amount of other bids. "We're running out of options," she said.

"Yeah, we are."

Sara kissed her brother's cheek. "Thanks for listening."

"Let me know what you decide about the bid."

"I'll keep you posted." She headed to the car, where she found a text message waiting on her cell phone. Travis had invited her out for dinner. She texted back, suggesting they eat at her house. Travis agreed, offering to bring a pizza. Thoughts of Dominick and oil leases fell by the wayside as she drove into town. The only thing on her mind right now was dolling herself up. She might not be as glamorous as the women Travis normally dated, but with a little help from Maybelline, this country girl intended to transform herself into a double-take.

Chapter Eleven

"Mmm…heavenly." The aroma of pizza greeted Sara when she opened the front door.

Travis's dark eyes swept over her before he stepped inside and sniffed her neck. "Mmm…heavenly."

Rogue. There he went again—his words, his smoldering stares and heated touches coaxing her heart to trust him.

"Hey, Walt." At the sound of Travis's deep voice, her one-eyed boarder bolted from the foyer. "What's up with him?"

She rescued the pizza box from Travis's grip and led the way into the kitchen. "I put catnip in Walter's stocking and he's miffed he has to wait until Christmas morning to play with it." She put the pizza onto a baking sheet and placed it into the oven to keep warm. "How about a drink before we eat?"

Travis rummaged through the fridge and helped himself to a beer. He unscrewed the bottle top and tossed it into her garbage can beneath the sink. Sara poured herself a glass of wine, grabbed Travis by the hand and led him into the living room. They sat on the couch in front of the Christmas tree.

"Where are all the presents?" he asked.

"My brothers and I aren't exchanging." Once the ranch had hit upon hard times, holiday gifts had fallen by the wayside. She motioned to the two boxes beneath the tree branches. "The box wrapped in silver and red is yours and the other one is for Charlie." She'd purchased a handsome wool sweater for Travis and a china tea set for Charlie.

"Did you buy me a gift?" Sara teased.

"Of course." He surprised her when he removed a small box—the size a ring would fit in—from his jeans pocket and placed it beneath the tree." He returned to the couch, snuggling close. "I wasn't sure where we'd be celebrating Christmas morning."

Sara's heart kicked into overdrive as she stared at the gift. Did she dare hope there was a ring inside? "Where would you like to celebrate the holiday?" Her voice sounded breathless.

"In bed with you."

His head dipped and Sara caught the faint scent of beer as his mouth grazed hers.

Sara melted into Travis, her senses soaking him in—his taste, the smell of his aftershave, the low rumble in his chest when he moaned. There was no other place she'd rather be than in his arms. She curled her fingers around his neck, urging him closer.

His hand found her breast, caressing, squeezing, coaxing a soft moan from her. "I'm not hungry," he growled in her ear.

"There's something I need to tell you." She clasped his wrist, then moved his hand to her hip.

"Can it wait until you've been properly kissed?" He nuzzled her neck.

She loved Travis's gentle teasing. "How long does a proper kiss take?"

"A very long time," he whispered.

"Suddenly I can't remember what I needed to tell you."

"Good." His mouth settled over hers and Sara basked in the knowledge that Travis desired her as much as she desired him.

A few minutes later, after his lips blazed a path down her neck, leaving her skin on fire, he murmured, "You have now been properly kissed." He handed Sara her wineglass. "Okay, what's this important something you need to tell me."

"I've thought about what you said the night of the Oilmen's Ball and—" she sucked in a quiet breath "—I want you to know that I have serious feelings for you, too, Travis."

The corner of his mouth curved upward. "I'm glad."

She fought to keep a straight face. "You don't have to act so cocky."

"You make me feel...cocky."

Sara's face warmed. "You're a handsome man." She brushed a strand of hair off his forehead. "All your sexiness makes me nervous and—" *tell him the truth* "—makes me want you."

He clasped her face in his hands, his expression earnest. "I won't abuse your trust, Sara. I know you're not the kind of woman who jumps into bed with just any man."

Okay, so he'd guessed her M.O. Rather than make her feel vulnerable, Travis's understanding of where she was coming from reassured her that she'd made the right decision to give their relationship a chance.

"You're the kind of woman who needs feelings." He flattened her palm against his chest. "There are plenty of feelings in here just for you."

He kissed her again—soft and slow. "I've never felt this way about another woman, Sara. You're a first for me."

His words freed her fears.

"Say you feel the same way about me." He brushed his knuckled across her cheek.

"I want this...us to work out." Sara wasn't sure of the exact moment Travis had slipped past her defenses, but from here on out there was no turning back.

"I'm glad I found you, Sara Sanders." Travis kissed the tip of her nose, then relaxed against the couch cushions and held her close.

"What are you going to tell Charlie?" she asked.

"That there are now two very special women in my life."

"Your first Christmas without your mother will be difficult for you and Charlie."

The mention of his mother reminded Travis that he needed to ask Sara if she knew about her father and his mother having an affair. But as he stared into Sara's luminous brown eyes, all he could think about was her.

He was certain that what he felt for her was love—the real and forever kind. He didn't have to try to envision the two of them sharing breakfast at the kitchen table. Arguing over who got to use the shower first in the morning. Sitting on the sofa, watching a TV program. Sara was an easy woman to be with. Heck, Sara was just plain easy on his soul. "I wanted to talk about our parents. I found out—"

"The pizza's burning." Sara got up suddenly and rushed toward the kitchen.

Thoughts of discussing their parents' affair faded to the back of Travis's mind as he watched Sara bustle about the kitchen. His musings turned selfish and he wondered if he could persuade her to postpone dinner while he took her up to the bedroom to...

"The cheese is brown around the edges—" she placed the pizza on a cutting board "—but edible."

He held out a chair for her. After she sat down, he buried his face in the crook of her neck. Her sigh reached his ears, and arousal shot through his gut. "Thanks for having me over for dinner tonight," he whispered before retreating to his side of the table.

"As soon as we're finished eating, I'll thank you *properly* for bringing the pizza over."

"Does this proper thank-you take place upstairs in your bedroom?" he asked.

"As a matter of fact, it does." Sara's cheeks burned bright pink, and her sexy smile promised Travis a *thank-you* he'd remember for a very long time.

2:00 A.M.

Travis had crawled from her bed a half hour ago and returned to the Lazy River, but Sara remained wide-awake, listening to the wind howl outside the window. She stretched beneath the warm covers—little twinges and aches a testament to Travis's enthusiastic lovemaking. He hadn't left an inch of her body unloved.

His tender touches and whispered words convinced Sara that he truly cared for her. And she decided the only way for her and Travis to have a chance at their own happy-ever-after was to wipe the slate clean between the Sanderses and the Cartwrights. She and Dominick would have to come to a business agreement about the Bar T or Travis would become caught in the middle. Sara didn't want him to have to choose between his newfound family and her. And there was Charlie to consider. The little girl had worked her way into Sara's heart. After losing her grandmother, Charlie needed her grandfather and Sara did not want to jeopardize the child's relationship with Dominick.

Tomorrow she'd phone Cartwright offices in Tulsa and schedule a meeting with Dominick. After visiting Cole earlier in the day, she was confident that her brother wanted to do what was necessary to save their ranch. The money from a drilling lease would pay off the second mortgage and the outstanding medical bills, as well as invest in repairs to the property, preserving her father's most treasured possession.

A steady income would also provide long-term security when hard times fell upon the ranch—disease, drought and crop failure. Still, breaking her promise to her father weighed heavy on her heart.

Daddy, please forgive me. I tried to do as you asked, but if I don't work out a deal with Dominick, we'll lose the ranch and I know you don't want that to happen.

The phone rang, startling Sara. Thinking Travis was calling to tell her he'd made it home safely, she snatch up the receiver. "Travis?"

"Sorry, sis, it's your brother, Gabe."

"Gabe?" She sat up in bed, tugging the covers over her naked body. "Where are you? What have you been doing? Please tell me you're coming home for Christmas?"

"Whoa. One question at a time."

"Are you okay?" She hoped he wasn't calling because his wild ways with women had gotten him into trouble.

"I'm fine."

She waited for details, but only silence met her ears. "Where are you?"

"Colorado. I'm roping cattle for the Ace of Spades near Durango."

Fighting a smile, she said, "I guess rodeo didn't work out for you."

Gabe chuckled. "I stink at bull riding. I'm better suited to chase after bulls than ride the ornery beasts."

If she hadn't already made up her mind, Gabe's call would have swayed her. She didn't want to see her family split up because her brothers had been forced to leave the area to find jobs. Not even her father would have wanted her to put the ranch before family.

"We're not going to lose the Bar T," she said.

"What do you mean?"

"I'm scheduling a meeting with Dominick to negotiate a drilling lease with Cartwright Oil."

"It's about time you came to your senses."

"Let's not debate who has more sense in the family." Gabe liked to provoke her, but Travis's lovemaking had left her too mellow to care. "Since we won't be losing the ranch, you can quit your job and come home for Christmas."

"That's why I called. I met someone and I think she's the one, Sara."

Oh, no. Gabe had met *the one* three times before and it had never worked out. When push came to shove, her brother couldn't commit. "What's her name?"

"Letty."

"What does she do?"

"She's a waitress at Bud's Bar."

Another barfly.

"If it's serious, bring her home with you."

"Ahh…"

"Please, Gabe. I want all of us to be together for Christmas."

"I'll see what I can do."

"Good. Cole's got several ideas on how to improve the ranch and I'm sure he'd appreciate your input." Sara cringed inside at the lie. Cole and Gabe knocked heads on a regular basis. Cole never cut corners and Gabe opted for taking shortcuts wherever he could find them.

"You think Cole would be open to starting up a horse-breeding business?" Before now Sara had never heard her brother talk about the ranch with excitement in his voice.

"I don't see why not." Lots of ranches managed both cattle and horse operations. Raising horses would allow Gabe to escape his brother's shadow. "Try to make it home for Christmas."

"I'll give it my best shot. Tell Cole I called."

"I will."

"Merry Christmas, sis."

"Merry Christmas." Sara hung up the phone, then dialed Cole's number.

"What?" he grumbled into the phone.

"Gabe just called."

"Is he okay?"

"Yes. He's working as a ranch hand in Colorado, but when I told him I intended to negotiate a drilling lease with Dominick he said he'd be interested in starting up a horse-breeding operation on the Bar T."

"He's nuts. We've got all we can handle with cattle."

"Our brother needs something of his own to manage."

"What do you mean?"

"You've always called the shots and—"

"That's because I'm the only one who does the work."

"If we cut a deal with Dominick, there'll be enough money for each of you to run your own business." Sara intended to use her share of the extra income to renovate her Victorian.

"Do you want me to be there when you talk to Dominick?"

"No, thanks. I won't sign any papers until I discuss the terms with you and Gabe."

"Any more news for me tonight or can I go back to bed?"

"Go back to bed. 'Night." After Cole hung up, Sara stared at the ceiling. How ironic that the one man her father had detested most of his adult life was the very person who would save the Bar T and keep the Sanders offspring together.

"CHARLIE, YOU HAVE A visitor," Juanita called down the hallway after ushering Sara into the kitchen.

Instead of Charlie answering the housekeeper's summons, Travis appeared in the doorway. Hair rumpled and a pillow crease across his cheek, he studied Sara through groggy eyes. "Hi." The greeting rumbled in his chest—the sound triggering a flashback of the intimate words he'd whispered after their lovemaking two days ago.

She motioned to his faded T-shirt and pj bottoms. "It's almost noon and you were in bed?"

A lazy grin spread across his face. "Had an emergency at one of the wells yesterday and I didn't get home until six this morning."

"Coffee?" Juanita held up the coffee pot.

"Yes," Travis answered.

"No," Sara replied at the same time.

Juanita frowned. "Which is it?"

"None for me, thanks." While the housekeeper poured coffee for Travis, Sara asked, "Is everything okay at the well?"

"A break in one of the pipes, but no one was injured, that's the important thing."

"Did you have any plans for today?"

"Nope." His eyes sparkled. "Is there something you wanted to do with me?"

Sara blushed. "No, but there's something I'd like to do with Charlie."

Travis's mouth fell open and Sara chuckled at his forlorn expression.

"Who wants to see me?" Charlie burst into the kitchen. When she saw Sara, she smiled. "Hi, Ms. Sanders. Did you wanna see me?"

"Yes, I did, Charlie. How would you like to do a little Christmas shopping with me today?"

"Can I, Dad?" Charlie tugged on Travis's T-shirt.

"We'll stop and have lunch at Tina's Trinkets & Tea

House." Sara needed to reassure herself that Charlie had no objections to her schoolteacher becoming involved with her father.

"I gotta get you and Grandpa a Christmas present," Charlie told her father.

"You'd better." Travis tugged his daughter's ponytail. "Run upstairs and grab my wallet on the bedroom dresser."

Charlie raced off. Juanita handed Travis a cup of coffee, then retreated to the laundry room. Travis moved closer until he stood before Sara. His brown-eyed stare stirred butterflies in her stomach. He threaded his fingers through her hair, then nuzzled her cheek. She breathed in the scent of faded aftershave and coffee. "I heard you scheduled a meeting with my father this afternoon?"

"Yes, I did." She flashed a sassy grin.

"Good." He kissed a sensitive patch of skin behind her ear. "Now, invite me over for dinner tonight. I'll ask Juanita to make her famous chicken enchiladas."

"Ask Juanita what?" the older woman returned to the kitchen with a laundry basket of bedsheets.

"I'm having supper at Sara's tonight and I suggested your chicken enchiladas. She's never had them." He glanced at Sara. "Have you?"

Sara shook her head. "Beulah claims they're the best she's ever tasted."

The housekeeper smiled at Sara. "For you, I will make my enchiladas."

"Okay, I'm ready." Charlie entered the kitchen, dragging her coat on the floor behind her. "Here." She handed Travis his wallet. He pulled out several bills and passed them to Sara. "Ms. Sanders will hang on to your Christmas money."

"I'm gonna buy a present for Fred, too." Charlie poked her head around the kitchen door frame and yelled. "Bye, Fred."

At Sara's quizzical frown, Travis explained. "Fred's Dominick's old dog."

"When Grandpa goes out of town, I get to keep Fred in the house with me."

"Dominick's out of town?" Sara asked. What happened to their meeting this afternoon?

"He flew to Arkansas yesterday but he'll be home later today."

Charlie opened the kitchen door. "Bye, Dad. Bye, Juanita."

"Be good for Ms. Sanders," Travis warned before the door slammed closed. He hauled Sara into his arms and kissed her neck. "I've missed you."

The housekeeper had made herself scare once more, so Sara relaxed in his arms and soaked up the warmth of his embrace.

"Thanks for spending time with Charlie," he said.

"My pleasure." Sara kissed his cheek, then hurried out the door.

Once she and Charlie buckled their seat belts and drove off, Charlie asked, "Where are we gonna shop for presents?"

"Tina's Trinkets & Tea House."

"What's a teahouse?"

"A place that serves lunch and tea. Mostly ladies eat there and Tina sells gifts like jewelry, candles and collectibles."

"What's a collectible?"

"Delicate things that break easily."

"Grandma always took me to Wal-Mart to buy stuff."

"Tulapoint doesn't have a big store like that, but if we can't find gifts for everyone on your list at Tina's, then we'll stop at Gunderson's Drugstore."

"I wanna get presents for my cousins Luke and Timmy and Lily and Rose. Rose is bossy but I'm still gonna buy her something."

"Are your uncle Duke and Matt bringing their families back to the Lazy River for Christmas?"

"Yep. Grandpa says they're gonna be here soon." Charlie's brow puckered. "Do I have enough money to buy all my aunts and uncles presents?"

Travis had given Sara two hundred dollars. "More than enough."

"I used to only have to buy my dad and Grandma presents." Charlie sighed.

"What's wrong?"

"Grandma made a gingerbread house with me every Christmas. I told Grandpa and he got sad."

"Maybe he wasn't feeling well."

"Juanita said Grandpa was sad 'cause Grandma used to make gingerbread houses when she lived with Grandpa a long time ago."

Sara felt sorry for Matt and Samantha and all the birthdays and holidays that they'd missed with their mother. "What do you think your father might like for Christmas?"

"Grandma always got Dad perfume."

Sara smiled. "You mean, cologne?"

"Grandma let me wrap it and tell Dad it was from me."

Five minutes later, Sara drove into Tulapoint and parked on the street in front of Tina's Trinkets.

"This is a house," Charlie said.

"Ms. Tina grew up here, but she moved into a different home and turned this house into a business." Sara held Charlie's hand as they climbed the porch steps.

When she reached for the door handle, Charlie asked, "Aren't you gonna knock?"

"Nope. We can walk right in." Sleigh bells attached to the knob announced their entry.

"Sara, what a nice surprise." Tina waved from the dining room. "Find a table and I'll be right with you."

When Sara escorted Charlie into the parlor room at the front of the house, the patrons who recognized Sara nodded and stared. As soon as they were seated, Tina arrived with a water pitcher.

"Tina," Sara said. "I'd like you to meet Charlie Cartwright. You may have heard that her father, Travis Cartwright, is Dominick's youngest son."

Tina held out her hand. "Nice to meet you, Charlie. Welcome to Tulapoint. How do you like your new school?"

"Ms. Sanders is my teacher."

"She is?" Tina winked, then whispered, "I hear she gives out a lot of homework."

Charlie giggled. "No, she doesn't. She's really nice and my dad likes her a lot."

"Is that right?" Tina's eyebrows arched.

"I don't have a mom."

"I'm sorry to hear that, honey." Tina brushed a strand of hair off Charlie's forehead.

"That's okay 'cause when my dad took Ms. Sanders

to Grandpa's ball—" Charlie smiled shyly at Sara "—I said I wanted a new mom just like my teacher."

Sara sucked in a quiet breath. Why hadn't Travis told her about what Charlie had said?

On one hand Sara was relieved that Charlie approved of her being with her father, but the little girl's confession spawned a new fear in Sara. If things didn't work out between her and Travis, not only would she end up with a broken heart but so would Charlie. Sara's meeting with Dominick this afternoon was more important than ever. She had to make certain Dominick's intentions were honest and forthright—too many people would be hurt if they weren't.

Tina, bless her heart, changed the subject. "The special today is chicken salad with almonds." She turned to Charlie. "I make a mean grilled-cheese sandwich if you'd rather have that."

"I like grilled cheese."

"Chicken salad for me," Sara said.

After Tina walked away, Charlie swung her legs back and forth in the chair. "How come everybody's looking at us?"

"They're staring because you're a new person in town and we don't get many visitors in Tulapoint."

"Oh."

Sara sipped her water as her thoughts drifted. She pictured her, Travis and Charlie living as a family in her sprawling Victorian. Travis was everything she wanted in a man and she was determined to put her bad experience with Josh behind her and reach for the happy-ever-after she yearned for with Travis. She could no longer avoid the truth—she'd fallen in love with Travis.

Later this afternoon, she'd tell Dominick how she felt

about his son and granddaughter. She wanted to make it clear to the oil baron that she had no intention of causing a rift between him and his son. If the gift Travis had placed beneath her tree was indeed an engagement ring, then it was time she and Dominick called a truce to the hostilities between them.

"Ms. Sanders?"

"What, honey?"

"Can you keep a secret?"

Oh, dear. Sara hoped the secret didn't concern one of her students. "Depends on who the secret is about."

"Me."

"Oh? And you haven't told anyone your secret?"

"No."

"Why's that?" Sara asked.

"Because I'm afraid my dad won't want me anymore."

What in the world was Charlie talking about?

"I heard Grandma tell her friend Mrs. Kimble that Julie wanted me to live with her."

Travis had told Sara that Charlie's mother had walked out on them. "What else did your grandmother say?"

"That my dad would take Julie to court and win, because he had a really rich father." Charlie wrinkled her nose. "Is Grandpa Cartwright really rich?"

"Yes, your grandfather is wealthy, but money wouldn't necessarily prevent your mother from seeing you." Who was she kidding? Charlotte's threat had been a valid one. Money and power went hand in hand. "How long ago did you hear this conversation?"

"Right before Grandma died."

Which meant there was a real possibility that Charlie's mother would be in the picture at some point in the future. "Why didn't you tell your father about the phone call?"

"'Cause." Charlie played with her napkin. "Dad will make me go live with Julie."

"Why would he do that?"

"Dad's always working on the rig and someone's gotta watch me." Charlie's expression lightened. "But then we moved here and now I get to live with my grandpa and be with my dad all the time."

"Honey, you should tell your father about the phone call." Travis didn't need to be blindsided if Charlie's mother showed up out of the blue seeking visitation rights.

"But I don't want to live with Julie."

"You won't have to live with your mother, but your father needs to know Julie contacted your grandmother."

"If you say so."

"Nothing bad will happen." Sara squeezed Charlie's petite hand. "Your father loves you very much. I bet he's done lots of things to prove how much he loves you."

"He bought me a new doll after Grandma died 'cause he said I needed a friend to cry with."

Sara's heart melted.

"And once when I broke Grandma's favorite necklace, Dad brought a new one for me to give her."

Tina arrived with their food and Charlie exclaimed over her Christmas-tree-shaped grilled-cheese sandwich. After Tina refilled Sara's water glass, she left them to eat in peace.

"Ms. Sanders?"

"What, honey?"

"Can I stay in second grade next year?"

"Why would you want to do that? All your friends will be in third grade."

"'Cause then I could be with you all day."

Charlie might get her wish sooner rather than later. After Sara's meeting with Dominick in a couple of hours, she, Charlie and Travis would be closer than ever to becoming a real family. Then Charlie could spend all the time she wanted with Sara.

Chapter Twelve

"I didn't know you were home." Travis stopped in the hallway outside Dominick's office. He'd heard the back door open and close several minutes ago but assumed Juanita had departed after making the enchiladas for dinner at Sara's.

"I wrapped up my business meeting early." Dominick shrugged out of his suit jacket and placed it across the back of his desk chair. "I was pleasantly surprised when Sara scheduled a meeting with me this afternoon." He went to the wet bar and splashed scotch into two shot glasses. "Where's my granddaughter?"

"Sara took Charlie out to lunch and then Christmas shopping."

Frowning, Dominick handed a drink to Travis. "Is that wise?"

"Is what wise?"

"Dragging Charlie into this. The more time my granddaughter spends with Sara, the greater the risk of Charlie becoming attached to her."

Travis wasn't following his father's train of thought. "What am I dragging Charlie into?"

"Into this charade you've been conducting with Sara."

Charade? "What are you talking about?"

"Have you forgotten our conversation when you first arrived at the Lazy River? You volunteered to persuade Sara to do business with Cartwright Oil."

Travis remembered that day but his original intent had changed along with his feelings for his father's neighbor.

"I never expected you to take things as far as you have with Sara."

Shocked, Travis said, "You believe I used sex to close this business deal?"

"Isn't that why you came home so late the night of the ball?" Dominick waggled his eyebrows.

Time to set the record straight. Travis placed his drink on the desk. "Yes, I agreed to try to sway Sara to sell the Bar T or negotiate a drilling lease with Cartwright Oil. But the closer I became to—"

"I admit, son, that I was worried." Dominick waved his hand in the air. "I didn't believe you had the nerve or the guts to carry your plan through. I'm proud of you." Dominick raised his glass. "A toast."

"To what?"

"Subterfuge. You're a master at it." Dominick tossed his drink back in one swallow.

An uneasy feeling gnawed Travis's gut.

"You're responsible for my neighbor coming to her senses and realizing she can't best me. Once the legalities are ironed out, you won't have to pretend to be interested in Sara anymore."

"No, Travis, you won't."

Travis spun at the sound of Sara's voice and found her standing in the doorway. "Sara, I can—"

"Please don't." She shook her head.

"Grandpa!" Charlie skirted past Sara and raced across the room to give her grandfather a hug.

"Hello, Charlotte. I missed you." Dominick patted her head.

Even if Travis could find his voice, now wasn't the time to plead his case. Sara's stone-cold eyes warned him that anything he said in his defense would go unheard.

"I got you a Christmas present, Grandpa."

Dominick placed a protective hand against Charlie's back and smiled. Travis's daughter had the power to melt the old man's heart. "Are you ready to talk business?" Dominick directed the question to Sara.

"Before Sara discusses anything with you," Travis said. "I'd like to speak to her in private."

"My business is with your father, not you." Sara's chin lifted.

"Charlie," Dominick said. "Take Fred outside for a walk."

"Okay." On the way out of the office, Charlie stopped in front of Sara. "Thanks for helping me Christmas shop, Ms. Sanders."

Witnessing the painful expression on Sara's face when his daughter hugged her felt like a fist to Travis's gut.

"You're welcome, sweetheart. Have a wonderful Christmas."

As soon as Charlie left the room, Travis made a third attempt to plead his innocence. "Sara, please, I can explain."

"I believe your role in these negotiations is finished."

Travis turned to his father for help, but Dominick

stared out the window, keeping his back to the room. Feeling as if he'd been called out before he'd even stepped up to the plate, Travis headed for the door. "No matter what you believe..." He clenched his jaw. "You and I are not finished, Sara Sanders."

SARA STARED IN A TRANCE across the kitchen table as she listened to the phone trill for the umpteenth time. The answering machine clicked on.

"It's me again. Sara, please talk to me." Travis was back to calling after he'd stopped by her house an hour ago—with Juanita's enchilada's. He'd rung the doorbell for fifteen straight minutes before accepting defeat and driving off.

"There are two sides to every story, Sara." More silence, then, "Please, call me back." The dial tone echoed through the kitchen until the answering machine clicked off.

Eyes burning, she held another round of tears at bay. She should unplug the phone, but a tiny part of her heart thrilled at the sound of Travis's voice. She yearned to believe there was a logical explanation for what she'd overheard in Dominick's office after she and Charlie had returned from their afternoon outing.

Maybe more coffee would help. She poured herself a fourth cup and stared at the Christmas gift Travis had placed beneath the tree the night he'd brought a pizza to her house for dinner. Christmas was two days away but there was nothing to feel jolly about.

She had no one to blame but herself for her miserable heartache. After Josh's trickery, Sara should have been wiser and smarter, but Travis had pulled the wool over her eyes and worked his way into her heart, silencing the voice in her head that insisted handsome cowboys couldn't be trusted.

If only she'd kept Travis at a distance, but he'd lassoed her heart from the get-go. His betrayal hurt more than Josh's, because her feelings for Travis were deeper, richer, more intense than what she'd felt for Josh.

Even his lovemaking had swayed her heart. His callused hands—tender and gentle on her body. His whispered words and deep kisses portrayed a man who cared deeply for the woman in his arms.

Still, she was a realist and should have known better than to believe the long-lost son of Dominick Cartwright would want to spend the rest of his life with a boring schoolteacher.

One day you'll find the right man.

She refused to give up hope that somewhere out there in the world a nice, polite, boring man awaited her. She swallowed the lump forming in her throat.

What if you're wrong about Travis? What if he does have feelings for you and Dominick's the one who's been fooled?

Would she find a ring or a pair of earrings inside the gift box? A ring meant Travis truly cared for her and he deserved a chance to explain the conversation she'd overheard in Dominick's office this afternoon. Earrings or a necklace would mean that Travis's intent all along had been to use her to win his father's approval.

The sound of the front door opening startled her. The only person with a key to her house was Cole.

"You home, Sara?" her brother called.

"In the kitchen."

Cole paused in the doorway. "You look like hell."

"Thanks." She sniffed.

"I guess the meeting with Dominick didn't go well."

"Actually, it went very well."

"Then why are your eyes all puffy?"

"Allergies."

"It's December. Nothing's blooming."

"I'm allergic to Walter," she fibbed.

After helping himself to a beer from the fridge, Cole joined her at the table. "What kind of a deal did you negotiate with Cartwright Oil?"

"Dominick was more than generous." Sara figured the old man had felt guilty and embarrassed that Sara had overheard his conversation with Travis. "He reiterated his offer of ten grand per acre." Sara shrugged. "I told him to double it and he did."

Cole whistled between his teeth. "I didn't know you were such a tough-nosed negotiator."

With her heart breaking and her world crashing down around her, Sara had relied on her toughness and fortitude to keep her composure during the meeting with Dominick. She was her father's daughter after all and had inherited his stubborn streak and bullheadedness.

"What are the terms of the lease?" Cole asked.

"It's a five-year lease." Sara motioned to the legal papers on the counter. "We maintain ownership of the Bar T and they pay us four million a year in leasing fees."

"We're millionaires." Cole whooped then frowned. "What happens if they don't find enough oil to make it worth drilling?"

"Dominick doesn't believe that will happen but in the event it does, Cartwright Oil pays us ten million."

"And when the wells eventually dry up—what then?" Cole asked.

"They're responsible for capping the wells and restoring the land back to its natural state. The lawyer at the bank will look over the paperwork after the New Year."

"When does Dominick want to begin drilling?"

"As soon as the ink is dry on the contract."

"When do we get our first check?" Cole rubbed his hands together.

"The first check is going straight into the bank to pay off the second mortgage and the rest of Dad's medical bills. You and Gabe can fight over what's left."

Face sober, Cole said, "I've thought a lot about Gabe wanting to start a horse-breeding business."

"Having a change of heart?"

"Yep. I think we need to diversify. That way, when times get tough in the cattle business, we have something to fall back on." Cole motioned to Sara's splotched complexion and puffy eyes. "Are you upset because you believe you let Dad down?"

She shook her head.

"Dad would be proud that you didn't allow Dominick to walk all over us. And he'd be happy knowing that Gabe and I are going to work together to make the Bar T profitable again."

"You're right. Dad would be proud." At least her father had been spared from having to witness his only daughter duped a second time by a traitorous cowboy.

Cole thunked the beer bottle against the table. "So where do things stand between you and Travis?"

"We're finished."

"What do you mean finished? You said you had serious feelings for the guy."

"I did." *Still do.* In time, those feelings would fade. She hoped.

"What happened?"

"Travis turned out to be another Josh." The lump was back in her throat, and she swallowed hard before continuing. "Travis only pretended to care for me until I gave in and agreed to negotiate a deal with Dominick."

"No way."

Deciding she'd rather Cole hear the truth than the fabricated version that would spread through the grapevine, she said, "I overheard Dominick tell Travis that as soon as the legalities of the oil lease were ironed out, he'd no longer have to pretend to be interested in me."

"Did Travis give you this?" Cole tapped the gift box.

"For Christmas."

"Open it," Cole said.

"I'm afraid." She pushed the jewelry box across the table. "You open it." Sooner or later she had to find out what was inside.

After undoing the pink ribbon, Cole removed a black velvet jeweler's case from inside the box. Sara held her breath, watching her brother's face. His eyes widened, then his face paled.

"What is it?" Sara asked.

Cole turned the box toward her.

A ring! She lifted the pear-shaped emerald from the satin cloth and slid it over her finger. "It's beautiful." Did this mean Travis really cared for her? That she had misjudged him? Her heart raced with hope. "What's the matter, Cole? You look like you've seen a ghost."

"I recognize the ring."

"How could you?"

Cole rested his head in his hands. "You weren't even born yet, but I was ten when Mom and Dad had a huge fight."

"About what?"

Cole nodded to Sara's hand. "That ring."

"I don't understand."

"Dad came home one afternoon and Mom met him at the door. I was sitting at the dining-room table, doing homework. I overheard Mom ask Dad where he'd gotten the ring she'd found in his pants pocket when she'd done the laundry. Curious, I spied on them. That's when I saw Mom hold up the ring. Dad told her to give it back and mind her own business." Cole left the table and stared out the window above the kitchen sink. "Mom accused Dad of having an affair. At the time I didn't know what the word *affair* meant."

Sara's head spun. "Oh, God." As if scenes from a movie were being fast-forwarded out of sequence in front of her eyes, Sara's mind filled in the missing pieces of a puzzle that had plagued her for years. "Daddy slept with Charlotte Cartwright, didn't he?"

"I don't know for sure. Her name never came up during Mom and Dad's argument."

"It had to be Charlotte. How else would Travis have come by this ring?"

"A pawnshop?" The look on Cole's face pleaded with Sara to agree.

"I never told you and Gabe because I thought it would just upset you," Sara said.

"Told us what?"

"Those last few days of Dad's life when he'd drifted in and out of consciousness, he called Charlotte's name." Dear God, her father had been in love with Dominick's wife.

"Shit." Cole sank onto the kitchen chair and stared into space.

Sara's memory drifted to the evening Travis had tried to tell her something but the smell of burning pizza had interrupted them. Had Travis already known about their parents' affair? If so, then why would he give her the ring?

Tears escaped her eyes, but she brushed them away. For years she'd resented Dominick's bullying attitude toward her father, but all along it had been justified. Her father was partly to blame for the terrible relations between the two families. The affair had ruined Dominick's marriage. Had taken Samantha and Matt's mother away from them. Had left Travis to grow up without a father. And had caused Sara's mother great pain.

The one man she'd looked up to all her life, had cared for during his finals days on earth and had vowed to carry out his dying wishes had disappointed her deeply. She had so many questions...and Dominick was the only person left alive with the answers.

"HEY KIDDO, WHAT'S UP?" Travis injected as much enthusiasm as possible into the question when Charlie rushed into the barn. The Cartwright clan had descended upon the Lazy River early that morning and after lunch Travis had retreated to the barn to escape the chaos in the house. And to devise a game plan for winning Sara back.

"Grandpa wants you to be with the family." Charlie climbed atop a hay bale and stretched out on her stomach. She stared him in the eye. "Are you mad at Grandpa?"

"Why? Did he say I was?"

Charlie nodded. "Grandpa said he made a mistake. Did he?"

Yeah, he made a big one. "Sort of."

The more Travis thought about the past few weeks, the more confused he'd become. Yes, he remembered wanting to impress his father when he and Charlie had first arrived at the ranch. Travis had intended to show the old man that, despite lacking a college degree, he had valuable experience in the oil industry that Dominick couldn't afford to dismiss. Travis had looked forward to convincing Sara to do business with Cartwright Oil. But after he'd gotten to know her better, his motivation for being with her turned personal.

In the beginning his desire to impress his father had urged him to find ways to be with Sara, but it hadn't taken long for the schoolteacher to secure a place for herself in his heart. His initial goal of swaying Sara to negotiate with his father had taken a backseat to swaying her to spend time with him.

"Are you gonna forgive Grandpa?"

The odd note in his daughter's voice caught Travis's attention. "Why do you ask?"

Her slim shoulders shrugged. "'Cause I gotta tell you a secret and you might be mad at me, too."

"Did you break something in Grandpa's house?"

Charlie's sober expression triggered an alarm in Travis. He sat on the hay bale next to her. "Okay, I'm all ears. What happened?"

"Promise you won't get mad?"

"I promise."

"Ms. Sanders said I should tell you my secret."

Sara already knew what was bothering Charlie? Why should that surprise him? Without a grandmother or mother in the picture, it was only natural Charlie would turn to the next most important woman in her life—her teacher.

"Before grandma died, I heard her talking to Mrs. Kimble on the phone." Charlie peeked up at Travis. "Grandma said she was never gonna let Julie see me."

"Why was grandma talking about Julie?" Travis asked.

"'Cause Julie called Grandma and asked if she could come visit me."

"When was this, Charlie?"

"Right after Grandma came home from the hospital."

"The first time or the second time?" His mother had gone through two rounds of chemo and had suffered setbacks with both treatments that had landed her in the hospital.

"The second."

Travis tried to summon enough energy to be angry at his mother but couldn't. He suspected that the knowledge she was going to die soon had made her want to keep Charlie all to herself for however long she had left to live.

"Dad, does this mean Julie changed her mind and wants to be my mom now?"

Heart breaking for his daughter, Travis stared at the glimmer of hope in Charlie's eyes. She was such a strong little girl and she'd never once shown any concern about

Julie abandoning her as a baby, but it was obvious as she'd grown older that she'd been wondering about her birth mother. "I'm not sure what Julie is thinking, but if you want, I'll track her down and speak with her."

"Are you gonna let her see me?"

"Do you want to see your mother?" Part of him hated the idea of sharing Charlie—mostly because he was still pissed off at Julie. Not because she'd walked out on him, but because she'd abandoned their daughter. No matter his feelings, Travis would do what was best for Charlie. His mother had selfishly kept Travis from the rest of his family and Travis refused to do the same thing to Charlie. Time would tell whether Julie could redeem herself in their daughter's eyes.

"I guess you can call Julie." Charlie scrambled to a sitting position. "You're not gonna make me go live with her, are you? 'Cause I don't wanna leave you, Dad." She wrapped her skinny arms around his neck and squeezed.

Most of the time Charlie was hell on wheels. Once in a while, like now, she showed a soft side and Travis treasured those moments. "We'll always be together, Twinkie, I promise."

She giggled.

"Charlie?"

"What?"

"I love you."

"I love you, too, Dad." She squirmed from his hold. "I wish you could marry Ms. Sanders, then she could be my first mom and Julie could be my second mom."

There would be no marrying Ms. Sanders if Travis couldn't talk himself out of the mess he'd made of things between them. He helped Charlie off the hay bale. "Let's go inside." He intended to drive over to Sara's and camp on her front porch until she agreed to hear him out.

As soon as they stepped into the foyer, Travis was greeted by Renée, Duke's very pregnant wife. "There you are." She shoved a glass of eggnog in his hand. Charlie joined her cousins in a game of Twister taking place in the family room.

Travis studied his sister-in-law. "You look tired."

"Don't tell Duke that. He almost canceled our flight today because of the baby."

"You weren't supposed to fly."

"No. But this is Timmy's first Christmas with his cousins and I didn't want him to miss out on the fun."

Renée was a lot like Sara—putting others before herself. Travis grabbed her elbow and escorted her to the couch in the front parlor. He placed a throw pillow on top of the coffee table for Renée to rest her feet on.

"Typical Cartwright male."

"How's that?"

"Bossy, yet compassionate."

Travis grinned.

"The Cartwrights are a fascinating family," Renée said. "And your sudden appearance after all these years only adds to their intrigue."

Travis switched the subject back to his sister-in-law. "When's the little Dalton due?"

"The second week in January, but I'm guessing earlier."

"How does Timmy feel about having a sister or brother?"

"Truthfully, I think he's relieved Duke and I won't be able to focus all our attention on him. After the surgery to repair his club foot we hovered too much. Duke wouldn't allow Timmy to participate in any sports until long after he'd received the okay from his physician." Renée sighed. "It's difficult not to be overprotective."

"Does Timmy like horses?" Travis asked.

Renée rolled her eyes. "Detroit doesn't have horses. Timmy wants to play ice hockey, but Duke's worried he'll injure his foot, so he signed our son up for the swim team." She laughed. "I think it's only a matter of time before Timmy plays hockey, because Duke's become a huge Red Wings fan.

"How's Charlie adjusting to Oklahoma?" Renée asked.

"Having family around has really helped her cope with her grandmother's death."

"How are you coping?"

"Asking as a social worker or a sister-in-law?"

Renée smiled. "Both."

"I'm good." Accepting his mother's death was easy— her betrayal, not so much.

Matt and Samantha entered the room. "There you are," Samantha spoke to Renée. "Amy needs your advice in the kitchen."

Matt held out a hand and assisted Renée to her feet.

"Something sure smells good." She waddled from the room.

As soon as their sister-in-law was out of earshot, Matt whispered, "Duke said she's been eating everything in sight lately."

The comment earned him a whack on the shoulder from Samantha. "Be nice." She took Renée's spot on the couch and Matt sat next to her.

"You and Charlie should visit Idaho," Matt said. "Amy and I remodeled the farmhouse, so now all the toilets flush and the showers don't leak."

Travis chuckled, noticing that he was becoming more relaxed around his siblings. "Maybe we'll accept your invite next summer."

"Yeah, I'd wait until winter passes. It's damned cold there right now."

Seconds ticked by, then Matt and Samantha exchanged worried glances. Something was up. "What?" Travis asked.

"Juanita mentioned there was trouble between you, Sara and Dad yesterday," Samantha said.

Trouble? All hell had broken loose.

"If my mother had taken me away from all this—" Matt spread his arms out wide. "—I'd be pissed, too."

"I'm not mad," Travis said. "Just deeply disappointed in our mother."

"You should be," Samantha insisted. "You were denied all the opportunities and advantages Matt and I received."

"I'm making up for lost time." Travis shrugged. "Dominick's giving me a chance to prove myself at Cartwright Oil."

"You like toeing the line for the old man?"

"I never thought I'd take to working on the mainland, but it's been a good change for both Charlie and me."

"So Oklahoma is becoming home?"

Once he convinced Sara to marry him, Tulapoint would be home. "You could say that."

"What do you plan to do with your trust fund?" Samantha asked Travis.

"I haven't decided yet if I'm going to accept the

money. I'm partial to earning my paycheck the old-fashioned way."

"We all earn our own way, Travis. That's not the point. The money in our trust funds comes from our great-grandfather's first gusher," Matt said. "The inheritance was passed down to our grandfather and then Dad got it all, since he was an only child. He divided the funds into two accounts for Samantha and me, then later created a third account for Duke. Now, there'll be another one for you."

"The reason I tracked down Dominick was to make sure Charlie had family to care for her if anything ever happened to me." That he'd found a place for himself at Cartwright Oil and fell in love with Sara was icing on the cake.

"Humor the old man and accept the money," Matt said. "Dad can't take back all the years you grew up without a father."

Matt was right. No one could reverse anything that had happened in the past.

Samantha changed the subject. "Dad said you convinced the Sanders to negotiate a drilling lease with Cartwright Oil."

"Dad's been trying to do that since before Jake Sanders died." Admiration echoed in Matt's voice.

Travis wasn't sure now was the best time to discuss their mother's infidelity, but he wanted the subject out in the open so they could deal with it, then move on as a family. "There's something you need to know about our mother and Sara's father."

Matt's eyes widened and Travis suspected his older brother had an idea of what Travis was about to say, since he already knew his mother had had an affair. But

Travis worried about revealing the truth to Samantha, especially after Dominick expressed a concern about her memory. He hoped he wasn't making a mistake in bringing up the past.

"The night of the Oilmen's Ball, I got back to the ranch around three in the morning and Dominick was waiting up for me in the kitchen. We exchanged a few words and I accused Dominick of being at fault for my mother leaving him." Travis rubbed his brow. "Dominick finally told me the truth about what happened between them."

"I can't remember." Samantha tugged Matt's shirt-sleeve. "Did Dad ever tell us why Charlotte left?"

When Matt remained silent, Travis told the story. "She had an affair with Jake Sanders."

Samantha pressed her fingertips to her mouth as tears welled in her eyes.

Matt's face paled. "I knew about the affair but not with whom. Are you sure you heard right?"

"Yes."

"I don't understand how Dad kept the affair between Charlotte and Jake from going public," Matt said. "That kind of news spreads like wildfire."

"What else did Dad say?" Samantha asked.

"That Jake Sanders had intended to leave his family and go off with Charlotte but right around that time his wife, Mary, turned up pregnant with Sara, so he stayed."

"I wish Dad had told us the truth." Matt shook his head in disbelief. "No wonder he's always had it out for Sanders."

"Mom never mentioned Jake's name to me and there

was never another man in her life that I knew of. I think she believed Jake would one day come for her."

"Do Sara and her brothers know?" Samantha whispered.

"I haven't had a chance to ask Sara yet." If she continued to refuse to speak to him, Travis might never get the opportunity.

"It's all so sad." Samantha wiped away a tear that escaped her eye. "I think Dad would have forgiven Charlotte if she'd come back."

"He never would have been able to trust her with Jake Sanders living next door," Matt said.

Right then, the doorbell rang and feminine voices rose in the hallway—Travis identified one as Sara's. A shot of adrenaline coursed through his bloodstream as he rushed into the hall.

"Sara?" He'd been trying to make contact with her for the past twenty-four hours and here she stood a few feet away.

"Hello, everyone." Sara's gaze remained glued to Travis. "May I speak to you and your father in private?"

Travis studied Sara's lovely but worried face. She'd curled her hair and made up her eyes the same as she'd done the evening of the ball. She looked feminine in her long suede skirt and silky blouse. He yearned to take her in his arms and kiss her.

God, he'd missed her.

"Dominick's in his office." He grasped her elbow—because he desperately needed to touch her—and led her to the office. He knocked twice on the door, then stepped inside. "Sara has something she'd like to speak to us about."

As soon as Dominick glanced up from the paperwork on his desk, he sucked in a harsh breath. "Where did you get that ring?"

Travis followed his father's gaze and for the first time noticed his mother's emerald on her finger. His heart flipped upside down. Sara intended to give him a second chance.

Chapter Thirteen

Dominick stared long and hard at the ring. "She kept it all those years."

"I don't remember Mom ever taking off the ring, except when she went into the hospital for the last time," Travis said.

"My father gave Charlotte this ring, didn't he?" Sara's voice quivered.

"Yes." The word escaped Dominick in a choked whisper.

"My God, Sara. I didn't know Mom's ring came from your father." Travis shook his head. "I never would have…"

"Never would have what?" Sara asked.

"Given it to you as an engagement ring. The emerald was my mother's most treasured possession. I wanted the woman I intended to spend the rest of my life with to wear it."

Tears welled in Sara's eyes. "I never knew about their affair, but Cole recognized the ring." She rubbed her finger over the polished jewel. "My brother over-heard our parents arguing. He caught a glimpse of the ring when my mother confronted my father with it. The woman's name my father had an affair with was never spoken out loud, but I should have guessed." Sara shifted her attention to Dominick. "My father called out for Charlotte right before he died."

Dominick aged ten years before Travis's eyes. His father's straight posture slumped as he left his desk chair. "When I learned about the affair, I asked Charlotte to return the ring to Jake. She refused."

"Now I understand why you're determined to own the Bar T." Sara didn't flinch under Dominick's sober stare. "Revenge."

Standing in front of the office windows, Dominick's agonized expression reflected in the glass.

"My father was partly to blame for Matt and Samantha growing up without a mother," Sara said. "And for keeping Travis from the rest of your family."

Motioning for Sara and Travis to sit on the couch, Dominick said, "When I discovered Charlotte had been seeing Jake behind my back, I gave her an ultimatum— if she didn't end the affair, I'd divorce her and make sure she didn't get one penny of Cartwright money or custody of Matt and Sam." He stubbed the toe of his boot against the carpet. "I also told her she'd have to leave Oklahoma."

"That's why Mom settled in Houston," Travis said.

Dominick nodded. "She chose Jake over me and her children and packed her bags."

"It's difficult to accept that the man I admired and loved all my life betrayed my mother in the worst way." Sara sniffed. "All this time I fought Cartwright Oil tooth and nail over the Bar T, because I assumed my father had been the one wronged."

"I believe Charlotte and Jake truly loved each other—that it wasn't a simple affair," Dominick said.

"But your father did the right thing—he sacrificed his own happiness and stayed with your mother when she discovered she was expecting you."

Travis grasped Sara's hand. "All those years my mother held out hope that your father would come for her."

"After my mother passed away, my father was free to track Charlotte down. Why didn't he?"

"I don't know. Maybe Jake figured Charlotte would want nothing to do with him after he chose his family over her." Dominick rubbed his hands down his face. "I've had trouble letting go of the past." His mouth curved at one corner. "Oil is in my blood and I don't need much of an excuse to pursue an opportunity when I see one. I wanted to take something of your father's because he took something of mine." Dominick dropped his gaze to the floor. "We all behaved badly."

"Sara." Travis squeezed her hand tighter. "Please give me a chance to explain the conversation you overheard between me and my father." He breathed a sigh of relief at her nod. "When I first arrived in Tulapoint, I was eager to prove myself to Dominick and find a way to fit in with my siblings. I saw a chance when my father suggested I try to convince you to negotiate a deal with him."

"I don't blame you—"

"Let me finish." He trailed a finger over the curve of her ear. "As I got to know you, I began to admire you. Pretty soon I lost track of my mission and found myself wanting to spend more and more time with you, because, you accepted me for who I was—a roughneck. I never felt that I had to prove myself to you, Sara. Before I knew it, I was falling in love with you. Not until yesterday did I realize how far I'd strayed from my original goal."

When Sara didn't speak, fear gripped Travis and he turned to his father. "Sara's the best thing that's ever happened to me. You weren't there for me all those years when I was growing up. But you're here for me now, Dad. I need Sara. She makes me happy. She makes Charlie happy. Give us your blessing."

"Travis, that's not fair to ask your father—"

"Don't speak for me, young lady," Dominick cut in. "I admit I made mistakes in the past, Travis. I should have gone after your mother. If I had tried to work things out with her, your life would have been different—but maybe not better."

"What do you mean?" Travis asked.

"I doubt you would have become the man you are today had you been raised at the Lazy River. You've had a rougher upbringing than your brother or sister, but you've become a man any father would be proud to claim as his son. Because of you, I've finally realized that family—not oil—should always come first." Dominick spoke to Sara next.

"Travis loves you. Charlie loves you. The three of you deserve to be a family. You and Travis shouldn't have to pay a price for your parents' mistakes. I'm getting old, young lady. I want my family together and at peace during my remaining years. If you don't marry my son, he'll take my granddaughter and leave."

Sara wiped a tear that leaked from her eye.

"You do love my son, don't you?" Dominick asked.

"I love Travis very much and Charlie, too."

"Good. Your marriage will be a new beginning for

both families. The past will finally be laid to rest and I, for one, will be glad to let go of it."

"I want you to wear this ring." Dominick grasped Sara's hand. "Let it remind all of us that forgiveness is the greatest gift of all."

"If you can find it in your heart to forgive me for being a bully all these years, I'd be honored to have you join our family." Dominick's eyes became overly bright.

A warm rush of affection filled Sara. Life with the oil baron as a father-in-law wouldn't be easy, but deep down he possessed a good soul and a loving heart.

"I'll let you close the deal, son." Dominick left the office, shutting the door behind him.

Travis dropped to one knee on the floor and grasped Sara's hand. "I love you with all my heart. Charlie and I want a future with you. Will you marry us, Sara?"

Sara's heart somersaulted in her chest. If ever she had a doubt about this man's love for her, he'd put it to rest with his next words.

"I can live my life without a mother. Without a father or siblings or a drop of oil money, but I can't live without you, Sara. You make me want to be a better man and a better father to Charlie. Take a chance on me and I'll spend the rest of my days making you happy."

Tears dripped down her cheeks. "Yes," she whispered. "I'll take a chance on you, Travis Cartwright."

He pulled Sara into his arms and kissed her…would have continued kissing her if not for the loud knock on the door.

Amy poked her head into the room. "Is Sara staying for supper?"

"Yes," Travis said, keeping Sara tucked against his side. "We have an announcement to make."

Amy's eyes lit up. "Oh, I love announcements." She hurried away, calling out to Renée to add another place setting at the dining-room table.

SUPPER WAS A LIVELY affair at the Cartwright household and Sara enjoyed every minute. A quilt had been laid out at the end of the dining room for the children to picnic on the floor. Refusing help from the women, Juanita placed several platters of food on the table. Amy put herself in charge of fixing plates for the children while the adults took their seats at the table. Everything seemed perfect—the food, the jokes between siblings, the children's laughter—the heated looks Travis cast her way between bites. When the dishes from the main meal were whisked away, Travis stood and clanked his fork against the side of his water glass.

After the room quieted, Travis winked at Sara and she knew this was the big moment. "I have an announcement to make."

Matt grinned. Duke's eyebrows shot up to his hairline. Renée and Amy exchanged smiles. Dominick looked smug. The kids ignored the adults until Charlie noticed her father and shushed her cousins.

"Before I share the good news, I want all of you to know how lucky I feel right at this moment. I thought I knew what family was...until my mother—" Travis sent his daughter a sad smile "—and Charlie's grandmother died. Then I discovered Charlie and I were part of a larger family." Travis made eye contact with Samantha, Matt and Duke. "I expected to be the outsider...the sibling that didn't fit in. The brother who brought back memories better left forgotten."

Sara's eyes stung at the heartfelt emotion in Travis's voice.

"That's not what happened. You've all shown me the true meaning of family. So tonight, I thank you for allowing me and Charlie to be a part of your lives."

"When I made the trip to Oklahoma, I never anticipated that I'd find the woman I want to spend the rest of my life with." Travis held Sara's hand. "Sara and I are getting married."

Wade clapped, and Samantha nudged him in the side. "Shush, Travis isn't done yet."

"Sorry," Wade mumbled, pushing his glasses up the bridge of his nose.

"I have everything I need now—a family, a strong, compassionate, feisty, beautiful woman—" Sara rolled her eyes, and everyone laughed "—to stand by my side." Travis smiled at Charlie. "And a daughter I love very much." Travis leaned down and kissed Sara before taking his seat.

Charlie's mouth dropped open. "Is Ms. Sanders gonna be my mom for real?"

"Yes, I am, Charlie. Is that okay with you?" Sara asked.

"Yeah, it's really okay with me!"

Matt stood and raised his wineglass. "To Sara, Travis and Charlie."

After the toast, Samantha said, "What about a Christmas wedding?"

"Next Christmas?" Sara sipped her wine.

"No, this Christmas."

Sara choked on the drink and wheezed, "Christmas is two days away."

"I'll phone Reverend Ryker." Dominick's statement caught everyone's attention. "I'll make a substantial donation to the church. He won't be able to say no."

"A Christmas Eve wedding. We can do it, can't we, girls?" Renée clapped her hands.

"I don't have a wedding dress," Sara protested.

"We'll call Beulah," Samantha said. "I bet her mother had more than one wedding dress. And we'll ask her to host the reception."

"I'll help Beulah prepare the food." Juanita poked her head into the room and smiled.

Bewildered by the Cartwrights' easy acceptance of her marrying into the family, Sara sat dazed. Travis tipped her chin up and stared into her eyes. "Say yes to a Christmas wedding."

"Yes."

"QUIT PACING, SHE'LL BE here," Matt said to Travis in the vestibule of the church.

The groomsmen exchanged anxious looks. At least Travis didn't have to wait and worry alone. Matt, Wade and Duke had all agreed to be his groomsmen and Cole was escorting the guests to their seats before walking his sister down the aisle. Gabe should have been helping Cole, but no one had heard from him. The church was packed—everyone in Tulapoint who hadn't left town for the holidays had showed up to see the last Cartwright son married.

Travis checked his watch for the umpteenth time. The ceremony was set to begin in thirty minutes and Sara had yet to arrive at the church.

"Are you sure she's coming?" he asked his father.

Dominick ran a finger beneath his shirt collar. "She'll show."

Travis had called Sara late yesterday and again early this morning but she'd rushed him off the phone with the excuse that she had too much to do. He'd tossed and turned in bed last night, worrying that she might change her mind about him and skip town today.

"Daddy, she's here!" Charlie poked her head into the church foyer.

Travis's heart beat so hard he swayed sideways, bumping into his father.

"My God, son, pull yourself together." Dominick's mustache twitched. "We can't have the groom fainting at the altar."

The groomsmen chuckled, then Wade suggested, "Travis, time to take your place next to the reverend."

Travis entered the church through a side door near the altar. Reverend Ryker smiled. Travis fidgeted, the faces in the pews blurring as he willed the doors at the back of the church to open.

The organist began playing the wedding march. Travis held his breath but the doors didn't open. The organist began the wedding march again and the guests in the pews shifted in their seats for a better view.

Suddenly the doors opened. Wade and Samantha led the procession down the aisle. Matt and Amy followed, then Duke and Renée. Once the adults took their places at the front of the church, Charlie, Lily and Rose shuffled down the aisle, tossing rose petals in the air. Luke and Timmy trailed behind with the ring bearer's pillow.

When the children were seated in the front pew next

to Dominick, the wedding march began anew and Sara appeared in the doorway with Cole.

"Wow," Matt whispered.

"Yeah, double wow," Duke commented.

"Behave," Samantha hissed.

Sara was stunning.

Travis's heart was beside itself. He wanted to see Sara's eyes but the veil attached to the headpiece hid her face. The ivory-colored satin halter gown was simple yet sexy—exactly Sara's style.

Cole escorted Sara down the aisle, and it felt like forever before they stopped in front of Travis. Cole placed his sister's hand in Travis's and said, "Make her happy. That's all I ask."

"I will." Travis squeezed Sara's fingers and smiled. Her lips curved behind the gauzy veil as Cole lifted it over her head.

"Dearly beloved, we are gathered here today…"

Before Travis realized it, the reverend pronounced, "You may kiss the bride."

Travis stared at Sara's beautiful face, soaking up the love that shone in her eyes—love for him. A peace settled over Travis. Today marked a new beginning for both families. He and Sara couldn't change the events of the past, but their union represented hope for a brighter future.

"Travis," Renée whispered. "Hurry up and kiss Sara."

Startled by his sister-in-law's voice, Travis did as instructed and kissed his bride.

When he and Sara came up for air, Renée muttered, "Thank God."

"What's wrong?" Duke asked.

"My water just broke."

Chaos erupted in the church as family members argued over what to do next, which hospital to take Renée to, who should drive and who would watch the children. Amidst all the shouting and panic, Sara and Travis stood at the alter staring into one another's eyes.

"I love you, Mrs. Cartwright."

"I love you, Mr. Cartwright."

"Looks like this will be a Christmas to remember," he said.

"One I'll always treasure." Sara smiled.

"Hey, you two coming or what?" Wade called from the back of the church.

Travis and Sara stared around the empty parish.

"The guests are heading over to Beulah's. The family's going to the hospital," Wade said.

"You want to go to the hospital or wait for word on Renée and the baby at Beulah's?" Travis asked.

"Let's go to the hospital."

"Are you sure, Sara? I want this day to be special for you."

"Being your wife makes every day special. Let's go find out if another niece or nephew is joining the family," Sara said.

Hand in hand, they left the church and followed the family to the hospital. The small clinic, staffed by a semiretired doctor and three part-time nurses had never seen so much excitement as they did when the wedding party arrived. Two hours later, Laura Rachel Dalton entered the world.

"Well, Dad," Matt said. "Looks like you'll need to set up another college fund."

Dominick grinned as he passed out cigars to the men. "I'll probably be broke by the time my children finish procreating." He narrowed his eyes on Travis. "See that you and Sara don't trail too far behind. I'm not getting any younger, you know."

Charlie wanted to remain at the hospital with her cousins, so Travis and Sara bid their goodbyes and headed to their wedding reception at Beulah's. "I feel like the luckiest woman in the world right now."

"Because you've got me." Travis smiled smugly.

"Yes, and Charlie and all of your family. I just wish Gabe had come back for the wedding."

Beulah's pink Victorian was lit up with spotlights shining on the huge sign in the front yard. *Congratulations, Travis and Sara!*

"Look, that's Gabe's truck!" Sara pointed out the windshield.

Travis parked in the back, then said, "I want to kiss you properly before we go inside."

As far as wedding kisses went…theirs was a gusher.

* * * * *

*Be sure to check out Marin Thomas's
new cowboy miniseries, RODEO REBELS,
starting in April 2011
with RODEO DADDY*

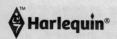

REQUEST YOUR FREE BOOKS!
2 FREE NOVELS PLUS 2 FREE GIFTS!

LOVE, HOME & HAPPINESS

YES! Please send me 2 FREE Harlequin American Romance® novels and my 2 FREE gifts (gifts are worth about $10). After receiving them, if I don't wish to receive any more books, I can return the shipping statement marked "cancel." If I don't cancel, I will receive 4 brand-new novels every month and be billed just $4.24 per book in the U.S. or $4.99 per book in Canada. That's a saving of at least 15% off the cover price! It's quite a bargain! Shipping and handling is just 50¢ per book in the U.S. and 75¢ per book in Canada.* I understand that accepting the 2 free books and gifts places me under no obligation to buy anything. I can always return a shipment and cancel at any time. Even if I never buy another book, the two free books and gifts are mine to keep forever.

154/354 HDN FDKS

Name	(PLEASE PRINT)	
Address		Apt. #
City	State/Prov.	Zip/Postal Code

Signature (if under 18, a parent or guardian must sign)

Mail to the **Reader Service:**
IN U.S.A.: P.O. Box 1867, Buffalo, NY 14240-1867
IN CANADA: P.O. Box 609, Fort Erie, Ontario L2A 5X3

Not valid for current subscribers to Harlequin American Romance books.

Want to try two free books from another line?
Call 1-800-873-8635 or visit www.ReaderService.com.

* Terms and prices subject to change without notice. Prices do not include applicable taxes. Sales tax applicable in N.Y. Canadian residents will be charged applicable taxes. Offer not valid in Quebec. This offer is limited to one order per household. All orders subject to credit approval. Credit or debit balances in a customer's account(s) may be offset by any other outstanding balance owed by or to the customer. Please allow 4 to 6 weeks for delivery. Offer available while quantities last.

Your Privacy—The Reader Service is committed to protecting your privacy. Our Privacy Policy is available online at www.ReaderService.com or upon request from the Reader Service.

We make a portion of our mailing list available to reputable third parties that offer products we believe may interest you. If you prefer that we not exchange your name with third parties, or if you wish to clarify or modify your communication preferences, please visit us at www.ReaderService.com/consumerschoice or write to us at Reader Service Preference Service, P.O. Box 9062, Buffalo, NY 14269. Include your complete name and address.

HARI1

JEMIMA yanked open a drawer in the sideboard to find Alfie's birth certificate. Her son was her husband's child. It was a question of telling the truth whether she liked it or not. She extended the certificate to Alejandro.

"This has to be nonsense," Alejandro asserted.

"Well, if you can find some other way of explaining how I managed to give birth by that date and Alfie not be yours, I'd like to hear it," Jemima challenged.

Alejandro glanced up, golden eyes bright as blades and as dangerous. "All this proves is that you must still have been pregnant when you walked out on our marriage. It does not automatically follow that the child is mine."

"'I know it doesn't suit you to hear this news now and I really didn't want to tell you. But I can't lie to you about it. Someday Alfie may want to look you up and get acquainted."

"If what you have just told me is the truth, if that little boy does prove to be mine, it was vindictive and extremely selfish of you to leave me in ignorance!"

Jemima paled. "When I left you, I had no idea that I was still pregnant."

"Two years is a long period of time, yet you made no attempt to inform me that I might be a father. I will want DNA tests to confirm your claim before I make any decision about what I want to do."

"Do as you like," she told him curtly. "*I* know who Alfie's father is and there has never been any doubt of his identity."

"I will make arrangements for the tests to be carried out and I will see you again when the result is available," Alejandro drawled with lashings of dark Spanish masculine reserve.

"I'll contact a solicitor and start the divorce," Jemima proffered in turn.

Alejandro's eyes narrowed in a piercing scrutiny that made her uncomfortable. "It would be foolish to do anything before we have that DNA result."

"I disagree," Jemima flashed back. "I should have applied for a divorce the minute I left you!"

Alejandro quirked an ebony brow. "And why didn't you?"

Jemima dealt him a fulminating glance but said nothing, merely moving past him to open her front door in a blunt invitation for him to leave.

"I'll be in touch," he delivered on the doorstep.

What is Alejandro's next move? Perhaps rekindling their marriage is the only solution! But will Jemima agree?

Find out in Lynne Graham's
exciting new romance
JEMIMA'S SECRET

Available March 2011
from Harlequin Presents®.

Start your Best Body today with these top 3 nutrition tips!

1. **SHOP THE PERIMETER OF THE GROCERY STORE:** The good stuff—fruits, veggies, lean proteins and dairy—always line the outer edges of the store. When you veer into the center aisles, you enter the temptation zone, where the unhealthy foods live.

2. **WATCH PORTION SIZES:** Most portion sizes in restaurants are nearly twice the size of a true serving and at home, it's easy to "clean your plate." Use these easy serving guidelines:
   - Protein: the palm of your hand
   - Grains or Fruit: a cup of your hand
   - Veggies: the palm of two open hands

3. **USE THE RAINBOW RULE FOR PRODUCE:** Your produce drawers should be filled with every color of fruits and vegetables. The greater the variety, the more vitamins and other nutrients you add to your diet.

Find these and many more helpful tips in

YOUR BEST BODY NOW

by

TOSCA RENO

WITH STACY BAKER

Bestselling Author of
THE EAT-CLEAN DIET®

Available wherever books are sold!

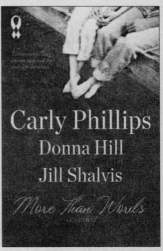

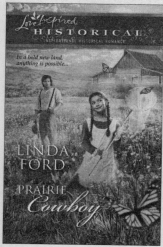

HARLEQUIN®
Super Romance

Top author
Janice Kay Johnson
brings readers a riveting new romance
with
Bone Deep

Kathryn Riley is the prime suspect in
the case of her husband's disappearance
four years ago—that is, until someone tries
to make her disappear...forever. Now
handsome police chief Grant Haller must
stop suspecting Kathryn and instead begin
to protect her. But can Grant put aside the
growing feelings for Kathryn long enough
to catch the real criminal?

Find out in March.

*Available wherever
books are sold.*